SAVAGE
BETRAYAL

The Nickie Savage Series

Book Four

R.T. Wolfe

Book and Cover design by eBook Prep
www.ebookprep.com

Cover photography by S.J. Jones Photography

September, 2016
ISBN: 978-1-61417-881-1

ePublishing Works!
www.epublishingworks.com

DEDICATION

I'd like to thank my husband, David, for his support and patience in living with an author.

THE NICKIE SAVAGE SERIES

Savage Echoes

Savage Deception

Savage Rendezvous

Savage Disclosure

Savage Betrayal

Savage Alliance

CHAPTER 1

The lights were out in the office. In fact, the entire top floor of the Northridge, New York police station was dark. Detective Nickie Savage sat at her splintered desk with nothing but the glow of her computer monitor to keep her company.

She hadn't been able to sleep. Her house seemed too big when she was alone. And since Duncan had taken their pup with him on his latest trip to L.A., the house was a special kind of empty. She shrugged and leaned back in her chair. She supposed when a client as famous as Johnny Lyons wanted to meet your dog, you brought your dog.

A zillion loose ends clouded her life. Two new cases sat in separate manila file folders on the side of her desk. Partner in the hospital; autopsy report on her latest case pending; stolen files to read…and who was the damned mole in the station? It all took away from her big picture.

Fu Haizi.

The child trafficking ring responsible for her abduction when she was a young teen. She'd fought her way from captivity. To freedom. And left the rest of the girls behind.

The peach Greek yogurt she'd had for breakfast threatened to return. Scooting her chair away from her desk, she dropped her head between her knees. This was not a road she could afford to travel. Not now. It never helped.

The grinding of an opening elevator door rescued her from her train of thought. It was followed by a flicker, then lighting of the commons area that was filled with vacant metal desks grouped in twos. Ignoring the cold sweat forming along her hairline, Nickie forced her head up so she could investigate. The telltale thump of conservative pumps on Berber carpet told her the assistant district attorney headed her way.

"Your lights are off," Miranda Vaughn said as she entered the dark office. Her hand reached for Nickie's switch.

"Don't touch that light. I sort of like you and don't want to have to break your arm."

Miranda snatched her hand back like she'd been burned, then marched over and glanced from the first of Nickie's guest chairs to the second.

"Just put the crap from one chair on the other." That was what everyone else did.

She complied and sat down, placing her briefcase on her lap. Even if her posture was perfect, Miranda's hair wasn't in its usual smooth ponytail, and her blouse wasn't ironed. Curious, Nickie half-wished she'd turned on the lights.

"So…?" Nickie prompted.

Miranda let out a heavy breath before placing her briefcase on the floor. "I couldn't sleep."

"Me either, but I ironed my shirt for the day." Or maybe put it in the dryer for ten minutes. Details, details.

"Oh, this." She glanced down at her soft rose-colored blouse, then buttoned the second to top button. "I didn't stay at home last night, but the couldn't sleep part came because—"

"Where *did* we sleep last night?" Nickie interrupted. She could almost see her blushing in the dim light and gave into curiosity. She reached over to turn on the lamp at the corner of her desk.

Miranda's chin dipped as she grinned. "Officer Parker's."

"Do you call him Officer Parker when you're…ya know?" Nickie asked as she flipped on the light.

"Ah, that's better. Thank you." Miranda sighed. "You look awful. The bruises are turning yellow."

Nickie raised her brows. "That tends to happen to bruises. Occupational hazard."

"And Dale's, I stayed at Dale's." Miranda lifted her head. "Ten years younger than me, sweet as can be, Officer Dale Parker." Her shoulders fell. "But the couldn't sleep last night was because of Eddy."

Nickie's partner. The partner who still lay in a drug-induced coma from the gunshot wound he took to the abdomen. Eddy would give her shit if he knew how much it worried her. She would never complain about any of her yellowing bruises from the last mission.

"Lynx, Vaughn. You're in a police station discussing colleagues. Call Eddy by his last name." It was downright wrong. "And call Parker Parker. Not Officer Parker and definitely not Dale." The last word stuck in her mouth like cotton candy. Leaning back in her chair, Nickie plopped one boot on her desk, then the other. "And you're rolling in the sheets with Dale but can't sleep because of Eddy?"

A grin spread over Miranda's sober face. "You mean I'm rolling in the sheets with Parker but can't sleep because of Lynx."

It all made Nickie's left eyelid twitch. She wouldn't give her the satisfaction of a response.

Reaching into her bag, Miranda pulled out her tiny laptop and set it on her legs. "Eddy may be loyal and driven, but he's bossy and arrogant. Officer Parker, um, Dale is sweet. You were right. He's the real thing."

Eddy got four adjectives, Nickie thought.

"I went and sat with him."

Nickie's head spun. "Which one?"

"Eddy. The doctors have kept him in this coma for almost a week now."

"You think he knew you were there?"

Since ADA Miranda Vaughn wasn't the type to shrug, she sat up straighter and said, "I have to believe that."

"Well, I'm among the first to be called when they wake him." Nickie's phone buzzed. She stuck her hand in the pocket and checked the caller I.D. It was from the station? She glanced around at the other offices surrounding the commons area to see if anyone else had showed up yet. Still no movement. "Savage," she answered.

"Mornin', Detective. Rickard here. Just finished the autopsy on Phillip Carson."

Phil the barber. Hide-guns-for-Fu Haizi Phil the barber. It was about time.

"Stop by anytime."

"I'm already here."

"You're at work early today."

"You have no idea."

The whole room had that formaldehyde smell. Plus, it was cold as hell. Nickie didn't know how Rickard could stand it. The ME danced around like he was in a rose garden.

The body of Phil the barber lay on Rickard's steel table. Two more stiffs occupied the other tables and some would be in drawers as the place doubled as the city morgue until funeral arrangements were made. Or sometimes not made.

Phil the barber. One Phillip Carson. Ghostly white and stiff. The gunshot to the abdomen was nearly identical to the one Nickie found in her partner's gut. The memory of finding Eddy nearly bled dry put that all too familiar lump in her throat. And stomach. And heart. The sight of him lying in the hospital bed. Drug-induced coma. What made him try to question Jun Zheng on his own? She should have known something was up.

"Nickie?" It was the voice of the ADA. "Are you okay?"

"What? Yes. Huh?" Oh, ME's lab. Dead body. Autopsy.

"You don't look well."

"Why, thank you, Vaughn," Nickie answered even though she deserved the jab. "What do we have, Rickard?"

Benjamin Rickard was the silent type. Kept to himself. Nickie could appreciate that. Before he began, he adjusted the collar to one of the neatly pressed plaid shirts he always wore. Nickie didn't want to appreciate that.

"Phillip Carson. Male. Age fifty-nine. Died from gunshot wound to abdomen."

And who hardly ever spoke in complete sentences.

"Blood loss did it. Hollow-tip bullet. Hands tied behind back post-mortem."

Wait, what? "What?"

"Yes." He adjusted his collar again. "See the color of his fingertips? White."

Yes. Chalky white. Ugh.

"If his hands were tied before he died, the fingers would have a purple tinge."

"A burglary made to look like a murder." It was the ADA. Nickie almost forgot she was there. "Isn't it usually the other way around?"

"Yes," Nickie agreed. "Backassward. Several large boxes had been stolen from the scene." No need for Nickie to tell the ADA she knew the large boxes contained guns. "Evidence was sparse but specific. Wide parallel scrapes along the floor, pieces of wood shavings. The place was wiped down too damned good, but we're counting on something maybe missed in the hurry. Forensics is still working on it."

A phone rang. It came from the only desk in the lab. "Expecting a phone call," the ME said, excusing himself and heading for it.

"Your desk is obnoxiously clean, Rickard," Nickie called to him as he made his way to the back of the room.

He waved a hand over his shoulder. "A compliment."

"But why murder him?" the ADA whispered.

Nickie took a deep breath. She had her theories, just no proof. And Nickie was a proof kind of cop. It's what gave her the track record she had. It was a rare attorney who could get past Nickie's evidence. "I'm going to find out."

"You know something."

"I think I know something."

Miranda rotated her body so her back was to Rickard. "Tell me."

Nickie wanted to share what she knew, she really did. But…

Miranda let out a long breath and stepped away.

This was why Nickie didn't get along so well with female types. Everything had to be all touchy and complicated.

"Don't give me that look, Nickie. I'm not simply a girl who's curious. I'm a friend. I'm an ADA friend which means I can help."

Now Nickie could add guilt to not being able to share what she knew.

Miranda waved her manicured hand dismissively. "I understand, truly I do. You're in a job that continually ties your hands behind your back. As a detective, you run into clashes over jurisdiction. Have you ever considered a job as chief? No." She stretched out the word as she answered herself and paced. "Too much detective testosterone drama to deal with. Maybe FBI?" She shook her head. "Red tape. CIA? Bureaucracy. You know." She stopped and faced Nickie. "You won't ever be happy until your efforts to save children take on more of a productive manner."

Nickie was speechless. And that was not an easy thing to make happen.

Something brushed against her back. The muscles in her shoulders tightened. Turning and jumping at the same time, she found the ME standing close enough that she could smell the onion on his breath.

In one hand, he held half of an everything bagel. With the other, he ripped off the sheet that covered Phil the barber. "See these abrasions? Whoever tied his hands post mortem tied them tightly. Why do that if the victim is already dead?"

Nickie should have been interested in what he was saying. She should have been more interested in how he got across the room so quickly. Or at least how he could finish breakfast while gesturing to a naked dead body.

But her focus couldn't leave the tattoo on Phil the barber's left forearm. It still had the raw pink markings around the perimeter, showing it was new. A falcon. Not the animated kind, but more like a photograph of a falcon in flight. Where had she seen that before? Her phone buzzed on her hip. She looked at the number. The hospital. "Detective Savage," she answered after the first ring.

"Good morning, Detective. This is Nurse Richardson calling to let you know your partner is awake."

CHAPTER 2

Duncan Reed sat in the single beam of moonlight shining through the window of his penthouse suite. The painting he'd started of Johnny and Bebe Lyons stared at him from the center of the makeshift studio he'd created next to the fully stocked wet bar. The Lyons were magnificent subjects, both physically attractive and photogenic. They deserved their tenth wedding anniversary painting to be of the utmost quality. And they deserved it sometime before their twentieth wedding anniversary.

Then why did Duncan have his laptop resting on his legs instead of his paintbrush in his hand? Because ever since Fu Haizi's Jun Zheng escaped jail, it had been this way. Duncan arrived at work—whether home or in L.A.—prepared his paints and brushes, then connected to the Net to search for answers about Zheng. Duncan believed that the guns found in the murdered Phil the barber's back room belonged to Zheng. And the files he and his brother stole from Zheng's accomplice's office? Useless.

Duncan had already discovered over a dozen media photographs of pedophiles and vice busts that contained Jun Zheng in the background. Photographs that helped Nickie connect with johns who had used Zheng's trafficked children. She'd narrowed down the fact that Fu Haizi had ten groups of children in captivity. Duncan felt for those children. However, his focus remained on his detective and her safety.

Nickie was not just his wife; she was the one person in his life who understood the curse that came with having a photographic memory. He didn't simply remember the violence he'd experienced as a child and during his stint in the Middle East. He could see, hear and smell the memories. Random images of the scars left on Nickie's back from Jun Zheng added to the clutter, making it as if pins pricked the back of Duncan's neck.

He opened a few more tabs, creating searches for vice busts in other states. He flipped through a handful of photos, searching for ones of Zheng. Xena rolled over in her crate, exposing her light-brown belly. The hotel manager hardly blinked an eye at the prospect of having her stay in the penthouse. Working for Johnny and Bebe Lyons had its benefits.

He opened a new search option, then bent closer to his laptop. On the screen was a new picture of Zheng. Duncan would remember the face even without his eidetic memory. The murderer stood in front of an upscale building with smooth concrete walls and tumbled edges. But it wasn't Zheng that caused Duncan to lean closer. The man in front of Zheng. The large man wearing a gray suit and black trench coat. Duncan's fingers gripped the sides of the laptop until it shook.

Nickie's father? Duncan stood, nearly flipping the laptop onto the floor. He set it on the wet bar and took three steps away, hoping the image etched in his mind would somehow change, adapt. He'd misunderstood. Been mistaken.

Rotating on the balls of his feet, he walked away before he stepped back to the laptop. The image hadn't changed or adapted. The photo may be grainy, but it was Jun Zheng standing in the background. Ramrod straight, hands folded in front of him, far behind a press conference. The caption under the photo read, "Assistant to governor of New York arrested for involvement in child trafficking." Duncan had aided with that take down, and had the scar on his shoulder from a gunshot to prove it.

Nickie's father stood only a few feet away from Zheng in the grainy photo. Duncan leaned in as if his eyes somehow weren't the 20/20 they actually were. He always knew her father was a bad man and terrible parent, but this? It could only mean one thing. His head tilted from one side to the other as prickles of electricity ran through him. Edward Monticello. He wasn't entirely facing Zheng. Coincidental encounter?

Shaking his head, Duncan stood tall. He looked down his nose at the photo. Experience taught Duncan long ago there were no coincidences.

How? Why? He went back to pacing. He had to call Nickie. No. He had to see her. His eyes turned first to the unfinished painting, then to the dog crate, then to his laptop. He pulled out his cell and made the necessary arrangements.

Hospitals all smelled the same to Nickie. A mixture of disinfectant bleach and some sort of ointment stuff. She'd stopped for some flowers. Stupid. They swung at her side as she took the stairs to the fourth floor.

As she reached the top floor, she rested a hand on the push handle of the hallway door. The flowers. What the hell? He wasn't a woman. He wasn't her lover. Worse yet, he was an ex-lover. Tossing them in a corner trash, she pressed open the door and looked for the sign that directed her to room 413.

The eyes of a few passing nurses landed on Nickie's badge. They nodded before moving on to their next room. The beat cop assigned to sit outside Eddy's room was standing in what she liked to think of as a drill sergeant stance. No chair. Knees locked. Feet apart. Hands behind his back. "Good morning, Officer…" She squinted as she read his name badge. "Corelli. How is the patient?"

Before he could answer, Eddy called from inside the

room. "Hey, Nick." His voice was strong for someone who had been in a coma. It was good to hear it. "I'm naked as shit," he said through the door. "Go get us some coffee. I'll get dressed. It feels like I haven't had any java in a week." And he was joking?

"On it," she answered and shrugged to the beat cop. Tracing her steps back to the basement, she glanced at the stems of the flowers and almost dug them out of the trash. What was the matter with her? She didn't know how to do partner-is-awake-from-coma; that was what the matter was. Warm and fuzzy, she was not.

The echo of her boots on the concrete steps brought back the image of when she found him in the stairwell that led down to the county jail. Lying there for who knew how long, bleeding to death. Why had he been interrogating Zheng without another officer or detective present? Without her?

Not that she hadn't interrogated Zheng alone before, but she hadn't been dumb enough to take him out of his cell. Alone. Leaving Zheng with the chance to take her frigging gun and shoot her in a stairwell.

As she reached the basement level, the flashes of Eddy lying at the bottom of the stairs became like photographs. Not like eidetic memory Duncan Reed pictures or anything, but enough to make her shiver.

She stepped around the imaginary Eddy Lynx and opened the basement door, heading for the coffee vending machine. The ADA was right. Eddy was loyal and driven. And bossy and arrogant. But he'd had her back enough times that she owed it to him to forget the bossy and arrogant.

Nothing could ever make her drink coffee, so she filled just the one auto java and headed back to the fourth floor. Before she made it halfway, a door above slammed against the concrete wall and was followed by the quick steps of feet racing down the stairs.

Placing her hand on her .45, she took it off safety and pressed against the side wall. What was it with stairwells lately? She supposed when you didn't use elevators, you got stuck in stairwell drama.

It was the beat cop barreling down the steps. Spotting her, his feet stopped before the rest of him, causing him to stick his arms out to catch his balance.

Her brows lifted as she waited for an explanation.

"Sir," he panted and looked from one corner of the small area to another. "Ma'am. I mean Detective Savage." Fire extinguisher to the right. Railing to the left. Poured concrete walls. What was he looking for? "Detective Lynx told me to come find you. That you had trouble."

Oh no. The muscles in her face dropped. She could only think of one reason why Eddy would tell that lie, and the reason was laced with deceit.

She took off up the stairs, forcing her mind to come up with other, more honorable reasons he might have sent the guard after her. Was he in trouble? Did he have something to hide? Was he the department mole?

Her feet halted. She didn't tell them to. The beat officer almost ran into her back.

"Detective?"

Squeezing her eyes shut, she kicked herself for letting her brain go back to disloyal thoughts. She shook her head and started up the last flight. The shuffling of several sets of soft shoes through the upcoming hallway did nothing to help her suspicions. As she opened the door, she noted the white-jacketed nurses and doctors as they rushed from one room to another.

He was gone. Eddy was gone.

He sent her on a dummy errand, then his guard on a wild goose chase so he could slip out. As she strolled among the panicked employees, she decided to give one last attempt at a reason for doing so and turned to the beat cop. "Was there anyone in the room with him when he asked for me to get the coffee?" Maybe someone holding a gun to his head, forcing him to do what he did?

"No, ma'am," the officer answered. His expression told her he suspected what she suspected.

"You were standing outside of the room. Are you sure?"

"I'm very sorry, Detective. He called me into the room and then told me to go find you." Corelli looked pained, but he added, "The bathroom door was open. No one was in the room or in the bathroom. He was alone, ma'am."

Nickie nodded as she forced her legs to move toward room 413. The charge nurse was yelling at everyone. She guessed that made sense. The hospital hadn't had that many patients placed with a guard let alone one who escaped. What was protocol? Not that Eddy had been under guard because he was a prisoner. It was for his safety. He'd been shot by Jun Zheng, who remained free.

For now.

Standing in the middle of Eddy's hospital room, her head beat out her heart. "That bastard," she said as she stood dazed with the rush of nurses and doctors going on around her. How could he do this?

"Detective?"

What did he have to hide? And why would he hide it from her?

"Detective?"

She'd been nothing but loyal to Eddy. Her feet started pacing, and her shoulders dripped with the weight of betrayal. His apartment. She would go there. Do a search. His office, too. Find a motive, and hope it wasn't what she suspected.

"Detective!"

Nickie glanced up and noticed the two nurses and the doctor she was trying to ignore. "People," Nickie said with as much authority as she could muster. "We have a Northridge, New York police detective on the loose who is recovering from a nearly fatal gunshot wound and drugs strong enough to keep him in a coma." They glanced at each other with gaping confusion. Nickie gazed from one side of the room to the other.

There. She found just what she needed. Officer Corelli. "The officer serving as Detective Lynx's guard will, therefore, be in charge of securing the area and of the debriefing."

The officer stared at her like she had three eyes.

"I'll be initiating an APB," she lied. This would be kept under wraps until she could figure out what the hell was going on. Regardless, all three of them barked questions and demands at her. Nickie ignored them, spun around and marched out the door.

CHAPTER 3

$\text{\Large A}$s she stomped up the concrete stairwell of the station, Nickie shook the morning drizzle from her hair and plotted her game plan with the captain. A warrant wouldn't be needed, she justified in her head. She wouldn't even mention the word warrant. Stick with your story, Nick. This was a missing person's case. Simple as that. A man left the hospital while under the influence of drugs that were strong enough to keep him out for close to a week. And, not just a man, but a colleague and detective of the department.

She would get permission to break in and search for him in his apartment. To confiscate his home and work computers. For clues to his whereabouts. To keep him safe.

And if she happened to find evidence of wrongdoing or that he was a backstabbing department mole reporting Nickie's every move to a paid source, that would be an accident and permissible in a court of law. Wrongdoing, she thought as she pushed open the door to the top floor of the station. What she suspected him of doing could hardly be classified as simple wrongdoing.

She stepped into the commons area, and all eyes turned her away. There was only one set of eyes she cared about. ADA Miranda Vaughn. Nickie dug in her heels, but made sure the ADA noted the slight nod in Nickie's head motioning toward the captain's office.

"Late start, Detective?" asked the desk clerk stationed outside of Nickie's office.

"Bite me," Nickie answered and marched past her still-dark office. Ignoring Eddy's dark office wasn't quite as easy. Her feet stopped and she nearly detoured for a quick look inside. Treachery scraped at her gut. A large figure came out of her captain's office, cell phone stuck to his ear. Captain Dave Nolan motioned to the both of them with his free hand. Get your asses in here was what it said. Uh oh. Without speaking, she and Miranda followed.

"I understand this is an unorthodox situation," he said into his phone, back facing them as she and Miranda sank into two of the leather chairs that sat in front of his desk. "However, a missing detective takes precedence over protocol. Officer Corelli is completely qualified to man the situation." Ending the phone call, he turned to face them and set his cell on his desk. No goodbye? It was good to know he was on her side.

"What the hell do you think you're doing, Nick?"

Or maybe not so much.

"Sir, he left."

He hated when she called him that.

"They've had him drugged up enough to keep him out for nearly a week. I'm worried about him. He must still be half-loopy. I'd like to ask permission to look for him. Break into his apartment if I need to. Search through his home and work computers."

"Just left?" Dave looked at her and tilted his head to the side. "What aren't you telling me, Nick?"

Nickie inhaled deeply, then let out a long sigh. She pressed her knuckles against her jaw, turning her head until her neck cracked, then said as fast as she could. "He sent me on a wild goose chase."

"Excuse me?"

She ran a hand over the top of her head, then grabbed the back of her neck. "I never saw him," she said like a confession. "He heard my voice before I came in his hospital room. He yelled from inside that he was naked and wanted coffee. I didn't want to see him naked, so I headed down to the cafeteria to get his coffee. On my way up, the officer standing guard at his door came tearing down the stairs with his gun drawn. Eddy told him there was trouble. Eddy told him I was in trouble."

Dave sat back in his chair and steepled his fingers. "He sent you both away so he could get away?"

Closing her eyes, Nickie nodded before she asked the question she was afraid to. "Do I need a warrant to break into his apartment?"

Dave dropped his chin and considered for longer than Nickie would have liked. "He was mindful enough to concoct this scheme."

"This is a missing person's case," Miranda interrupted. "A life is in danger. Detective or no detective, a person who is under the residual effects of coma-inducing narcotics cannot be acting fully of his own accord. There is no need for a warrant."

"Great," Dave said. "I have two women with a conflict of interest giving me legal advice." He waved them on anyway. She hoped she wouldn't ruin his trust in her.

"Let's go, Nickie," Miranda said. "I'll drive."

Nickie didn't speak on the way over. Her brain fought her. Eddy. The mole? What other reason could he have had to do this? Pieces started fitting together. Pieces she didn't want to fit together.

The occasional swipe of delayed wipers distracted her. It was a good thing. She didn't know what to say to Miranda. It wasn't like she was going to tell her there was a department mole. That someone had been watching Nickie and reporting her every move to an employee that worked for her father. The employee who was now six feet under. This had more layers than she cared to sort.

"You're quiet," Miranda said. "You're quiet, and something is off."

Nickie slung a boot over her knee. "How so?"

"A colleague. No, your partner. No, your friend is missing and drugged. He still has serious injuries, and you seem to have no emotion whatsoever."

Nickie glanced over and noted the black smudges beneath the ADA's eyes. It wasn't that she didn't care. It was more that she couldn't afford to. She rubbed a hand over her face. Any evidence of wrongdoing found in Eddy's apartment needed to be incidental. In order for that to happen, Nickie had to keep Miranda in the dark.

"He's my partner. Of course I have emotion. I'm focused, that's all." It wasn't a lie. "Let's go find him."

Miranda pulled into the parking space in front of Eddy's apartment. Nickie noted new paint around the front door. Or, was it a new frame altogether? Regardless, she banked it in her memory. She would not be able to take written or audio notes on this search. This wasn't an investigation. They were simply trying to find a friend.

The air was cool and the drizzle came down harder. As they exited the vehicle, Miranda pulled her suit jacket up and over her smooth ponytail. Nickie lifted her chin to the sky and let the water cool her face.

As Miranda hurried to the front door, Nickie rounded the back of the vehicle. She popped the trunk and searched under the mat for what she was looking for.

"What are you doing?" Miranda called from the cover of the front door awning.

There it was, Nickie thought, hand wrapping around cold iron. She didn't answer. Instead, she closed the trunk and slung the crowbar she'd retrieved over her shoulder. Heading around the car in the rain, she stopped when she got to Eddy's door. She stuck the crowbar in the doorjamb, but then realized she might not need it. Setting the crowbar on the concrete next to her, she pulled out her set of keys. Could she still have it? And if so, would it work? There it was. Her old key to Eddy's apartment.

Miranda didn't seem surprised. More like she was relieved that Nickie was no longer going to break down the door. Nickie hadn't used the key in years. Quietly making a wish, she sighed as the key turned, and the lock released.

Nickie knocked as she cracked open the door. "Hello," she called and opened it farther. Everything was dark. Shades drawn. "Eddy? It's Nickie and Miranda. We're worried about you, man."

Something smelled rotten. Fruit? Old pizza? At least it wasn't the scent of a dead body. Nickie was prepared for anything. "You wait here," she commanded Miranda. "I'm gonna take a look around."

Miranda grabbed hold of Nickie's upper arm. "I'm afraid I'm not comfortable with that."

Oh good grief. "He's still drugged. It's not safe."

"I'm afraid I'm still not comfortable with it."

Nickie didn't have time for this and stepped in with Miranda hanging onto her arm. The apartment was small. A single picture of Eddy holding a large catfish hung in the center of the longest living room wall. It looked like a postage stamp on a large white envelope. She used the short hallway to get to the small walk-through kitchen and noted stacks of dirty dishes that appeared like they'd been there since before he was admitted to the hospital. Wandering through, she checked the kitchenette on the other side. The small, wooden table with two chairs sat empty.

The short hallway also led to the only bedroom. Everything smelled like bachelor. He hadn't moved a single piece of furniture since the last time she'd been there. The place was as small as the townhouse she'd lived in before she married Duncan. And if she admitted it, was just as messy. She checked the closets, under the bed, and in the bathroom.

No signs that anyone had been there for days, maybe weeks.

Did he really have no one to come and take care of this stuff? And why didn't she know more about his life? A wave of guilt trickled through her. Or was the lack of history purposeful? Was it part of his cover? She had to quit hypothesizing.

Nickie looked down and noted Miranda still had hold of her upper arm. Tears streamed down each of her cheeks. "It's going to be okay," Nickie lied. She spoke the obvious. "He's not here. I'm going to search for signs of where he might be. I need you to get to the station and start looking through his office computer." It was the best idea Nickie could come up with. She needed Miranda to back up her warrantless break-in, and now she needed to be alone to do what was next.

Miranda nodded. "How will you get home?"

Oh, right. Miranda drove. "I know people," Nickie said and smiled.

Without warning, Miranda threw her arms around her.

Nickie's eyes almost popped out of her head. She held her arms out to the side. This is what Nickie got for being friends with a female. "Um…there, there," she said and patted Miranda's shoulder three times with her fingertips. It seemed to appease Miranda as she sniffled, nodded, then walked like a zombie out the front door without even closing it.

Nickie stood in the doorway between the bedroom and the master bath. Bed unmade. TV remote thrown in the middle of the bed. Bathroom empty. Toilet seat up, shower curtain open with a film of orange mildew growing around the edges. It helped that Miranda wasn't hanging onto her upper arm. She could go into search warrant mode. Well, minus the search warrant.

No signs of foul play, missing persons or that Eddy might be a mole spying on Nickie for her father's sake. She was his partner. If she had an ounce of social skill, she would have offered to take care of his apartment and none of this would have been necessary. Now, she stood wondering if his name was even Eddy Lynx. Her chin dropped. She would have Duncan do a thorough background check that weekend when he came back from L.A.

Taking a deep breath, she lifted her head high and continued. Clothes were strewn on the floor, and a few live rounds and a magazine were tossed on the only dresser in the bedroom. The clip was full. She could see the bullets lined inside from where she stood.

As if a search beam had been flipped on, light poured from the hallway behind her. In a kneejerk reaction, she took one large step and pressed against the wall inside the bedroom door. Miranda had left the front door unlatched. Wind could have swung it open.

Except, then why weren't her feet moving? Because she was executing a search without backup. Because there was nothing standing between her and the front door other than a short apartment hallway. She wasn't just searching for a department mole; she was also searching for a person who may be involved with murder.

She placed her ear closer to the hall, stopping at the doorway trim. She leaned over and looked with a single eye. The hallway was clear. Sliding her Smith and Wesson out of her holster, she took aim. With gun drawn and arms extended, she twirled around and faced the light head-on. Her knees were soft as she took a step, then another and another.

As she listened for footsteps or the creak of a floorboard, she watched for moving shadows. If there were even a slight wind in the midst of the light drizzle, she would feel better about all of this.

She could make it around the walk-through kitchen, then she would check the door from the kitchenette to the living room. Except, when she took another step, an arm swung around the opening from the kitchen, knocking Nickie's gun out of her hand.

Male strength. She ignored the rush of adrenaline and the prickling at the back of her neck. She was too damned pissed off. Before he had a chance to retract his arm, she grabbed his wrist, yanking him into the light and twisting at the same time. She used her weight to manipulate his body, forcing him to lose his balance. She dropped her shoulder and dug in, toppling them both to the floor. She landed on him mostly with her hip.

Hey, she knew that scent. Leather. The slightest hint of that kind of cologne that made her feel something between dizzy and a secure sense of home.

"Duncan?" She scurried from the awkward position she'd landed in and sat up, straddling him. "You're in L.A."

As he rubbed the spot on his collarbone that her shoulder had plowed into, he lifted his brows at her as if the fact that he was lying there made her statement ridiculous.

"How did you know I was here?" she barked, somewhere between still shook up and elated. "Who told you I was here? Why are you here?" Is that what the bruises on her face looked like? Because his had turned a deep yellow since the last time she saw him.

"Where is your car?" he asked in the almost-baritone voice she'd missed more than was reasonable.

"I got a ride."

"How were you going to get home?"

And just as she told Miranda, she said, "I know people," only this time with a smile that was sincere.

He nodded. "I need to talk to you."

Nickie gave him her full attention, but felt she needed to point out the obvious since she was sitting on his lap and all. "It feels—" She shifted just enough. "Like you want to do more than talk." The relief of having him here with her. In New York. To be with her as she dealt with all of this. Hey, wait. "You're in L.A.," she repeated.

"I need to talk to you," he said again as he guided her from his lap. Sitting up, he rested his forearms on top of his knees. The expression on his face read talk only.

"Aren't you going to ask me what I'm doing in Eddy's apartment?" she said.

Duncan shook his head. "I wasn't sure it was you." His tone. His face. She knew it well, and this time she wished she didn't. It was making her lose her train of thought, and sort of freaking her out.

"You're not asking me why my gun was drawn," she said as a statement instead of a question.

"I spoke with Dave. He told me where to find you." He seemed worn. Not the no-sleep kind either. "We need to talk."

CHAPTER 4

For nearly the entire plane ride home, Duncan had rehearsed this. Now, he was mute.

"So then, you know Lynx is AWOL," Nickie said as they sat on the hallway floor in Lynx's apartment.

"I have theories," he said. "What are your thoughts?"

"Things I don't want to think. Hospital video surveillance revealed still shots of him in three locations." She shook her head as she leaned back, sticking her legs out in front of her. "He'd had enough physical acuteness to get dressed in his civvies but was clearly in pain. The photos showed him gripping his wound."

Duncan opened his eyes only long enough for him to reach for her hands and take both of them in his.

"We can hypothesize the whys," she said. "The facts remain that he's been behaving oddly for weeks. Distant. Reclusive. He authorized the release of Jun Zheng for independent questioning and was shot with his own gun in the process. Left for dead?" She shrugged. "He didn't die."

"Nickie." He had to tread carefully. As much as Duncan didn't care for Eddy, this was her partner and likely another to add to her long list of people who had betrayed her. But for now, he needed to refocus the course of their conversation to his discovery regarding her father.

She continued, deep in her thought, as if he hadn't spoken her name. "Phil the barber died from a bullet from the same gun. Eddy's gun," she said as she pulled her hands from his so she could use them to gesture as she spoke. "Same spot to the abdomen. One dies. The other doesn't."

"Nickie."

"I'm not accusing. Just stating the facts we've got since it's all we've got. Both the captain and ADA gave me the nod to search for him. No warrant needed. Which is why I'm here alone."

He closed his eyes. There was a long pause where he pictured her head dipping from one side to the other, the way she did when she was animated.

"We might find something that can help him, or clear him of the facts that are not making him look so good."

He took her hands again, but this time by the wrists. He pulled them close and slowly opened his lids. "Nickie, I found something."

She rolled her eyes. "You're never going to get any work done if you keep spending all your time searching the Net—" She tried to pull her hands free, but he held tight this time. Her body stiffened and her gaze darted to his in response. "You're freaking me out."

"I found another shot of Zheng."

Unfortunately, her shoulders relaxed. "Not that I don't appreciate it and all, but somehow you've found enough of those things for me to get more intel on him than I know what to do with." She gave her hands another tug. His grip remained.

"Please don't overreact." As the phrase rarely had the appropriate outcome, it was also not included in his airborne rehearsal.

"Okay," she said in slow motion. "If you let go of my arms, I promise not to overreact." She glanced down at her hands. Her brows furrowed. A longer pause ensued as he watched her expression turn to understanding. "You didn't call me. Not before you left L.A., and not when you arrived in Northridge, not even before you made it over here." He read fear in her face and with good reason.

Releasing her wrists, they sprang back toward her chest. As he reached into the inside pocket of his jacket, he said, "Please keep an open mind."

"Right." Her tone did not sound accommodating.

He'd folded the picture of Jun Zheng and her father twice. It fumbled in his fingers as he worked to unfold it. Before he turned it to face her, he checked each of her eyes. He wasn't sure what he might find in one that he didn't find in the other. Her head tilted away from him, but her gaze remained on his. Even when he rotated the printed picture to face her, it was as if she feared what she might see.

They sat like that, likely for a few seconds, but it seemed more like several minutes until she allowed her gaze to drop to the photo.

Her eyes tightened around the image, but her hands did not reach for it. She opened her mouth and shut it again. As she fell back against the wall of Eddy's hallway, it was as if her body had lost all muscle function.

The steel gray of her eyes darted from one side of Duncan's head to the other, up then down. "But this means…" Her head shook in two short motions as if she was trying to free her mind of the inevitable place it led. "You don't think he…?"

With her gaze returning to the image, her hand reached out and she pinched the paper with her thumb and forefinger. Around her finger rested the wedding ring that symbolized the commitment he made to her for better or for worse.

Holding the print far away from her, she crept to a standing position. Her feet began to pace. "Zheng. Edward. My abduction," she said as she connected the same points he had in L.A. Back and forth she went, ignoring the fact that she had to step over his legs for each pass she made in the small hallway.

"My escape. The missing files." The paper crumpled in her hands as she ran them over the top of her head. It killed him to watch this, yet it needed to be done. Allowing her to cycle through, he pulled his legs in closer so she wouldn't trip as she paced.

Her feet finally stopped. She stood with her legs a little more than shoulder-width apart, knees locked. "I think I knew."

He rose from his sitting position and faced her.

Clutching the crumpled paper with both hands, she squinted at a spot on the wall behind him. "I think I knew," she repeated. "But why?" Her chin dropped. "And Eddy."

Yes, Eddy. "You have a point about your suspicions, but are you sure?"

"Of course, I'm not sure." She raised her voice now. "Evidence, evidence, evidence." It had been only moments since she'd stood, but her legs seemed to collapse and she dropped into his arms. He led them to the floor. "This makes my brain hurt," she mumbled.

He sat behind her this time, wrapping his legs around her as she melted into him.

"I'm not sure I can do this, Duncan."

"I am here."

Her chest expanded and released. "I don't know where to start. I never don't know where to start."

He wrapped his arms around her warm body. Her head rotated, her cheek resting on his shoulder. They sat this way for several minutes. With the shades drawn, the only light was from the open front door. Her phone buzzed. She ignored it.

He whispered as his lips touched her ear. "We could start with finishing the search here, where we are."

"Or we could move to Alaska."

"Excuse me?"

Her body twisted so they remained twined but faced each other. "Yes, Alaska. We won't tell anyone. Just you and me." Her soft lips rested on his cheek. "I bet there are girls that need to be saved in Alaska," she whispered. "And rich and famous people who need portraits painted."

Her lungs expanded and she relaxed further in his arms. He loved this woman.

* * *

Although Eddy's apartment was in disarray, Duncan attempted not to disturb anything. He didn't believe Eddy would notice if the February issue of Playboy was on top or shuffled down to number three in his stack of questionable literature. Nonetheless, he replaced everything back to its original location.

This would be easier if Nickie had given him specific items to search for. Regardless, he would have snapshot photos in his mind of each drawer, closet and room. She'd given him gloves to prevent compromising the scene. His appreciation of said gloves came, however, not in the form of maintaining the integrity of the search but from the condom wrappers—opened as well as unopened—that were strewn among boxer briefs and piles of random, unmatched socks.

It caused him to ponder as to why he would be the one searching the disgraced detective's bedroom drawers. He glanced over his shoulder and noticed Nickie standing at the only closet in the bedroom. Knowing everything about this woman, he recognized the stance and walked to her. Shoulders forward, head tilted upward, legs wide and knees locked. It read caution and apprehension with a touch of avoidance.

The stance didn't waver as he approached. He stood close enough that the slight scent of lavender that seemed to follow her everywhere wafted over him, causing his IQ to drop at least thirty points. On the floor of the closet, dirty clothing surrounded the perimeter of a single empty laundry basket. A lone shelf in the small closet was nearly as empty as the laundry basket. Except for a silver laptop that rested with lid partially open.

He knew where Nickie's mind had wandered. His did as well. Words weren't necessary. Instead, he stepped around her and reached for the machine. As he turned with it in his gloved hand, her head dropped in silent defeat. Her feet remained where they were, so he maneuvered around her and headed toward the living room. Before exiting the

bedroom, he glanced over his shoulder. Nickie had resumed her search, checking the pockets of the clothing on hangers as if the machine didn't exist.

The laptop booted up. Eight percent battery. While Nickie combed through Lynx's belongings, Duncan hacked around the password. She didn't check on him and hadn't spoken a word since long before the closet, but he could feel the tension radiating down the hall from Lynx's bedroom. This was her partner. The detective who worked side-by-side with her on dozens if not hundreds of cases over the past few years. A love interest at one time, although something that only bothered Duncan when Lynx used it in his favor.

She'd been betrayed by so many in her life. Could Lynx be yet another to add to the growing list? Five percent battery. Duncan had a charger that would fit this machine, but it was at home. He considered searching for one in Lynx's apartment, then decided on that route only if the machine died.

And he was in. Preferences to machine data to coding. He found a number of email accounts and…one of the ones used to report intel on Nickie. His fingers tightened enough to make it difficult to continue. The latest email. It was one Duncan had not found before.

on my way to the release. will rendezvous at meeting point.

Release as in the release of Jun Zheng. Duncan would kill Eddy Lynx. He would strangle him with his own two hands. His Nickie. His detective. Rage morphed into despair. Giving himself a moment, he closed his eyes and gathered the composure Nickie deserved. When he opened them, she was there. Words were moot. She read his expression. Damn it all to hell. He wasn't ready for it.

Nodding, Nickie craned her neck away and bit the side of her cheek. Her lids dropped, covering the glossy red as she said, "We have what we need. Let's get out of here."

He rose from his spot on the couch, then placed his free hand on her lower back. The muscles were rock hard, and they flexed and released as they marched to his car.

CHAPTER 5

Nickie decided not to argue about who drove. It was no use. She needed to make her game plan anyway. In between shifting gears, Duncan rested his hand on her thigh. It wasn't a sensual distraction as it sometimes could be. The warmth radiated a sense of peace from beneath his hand, down her legs and up her body. It made it that much easier to process the bombshells she'd learned that day.

As she mapped out the next few hours and days, her cell rang. Since it was the third time in ten minutes, she decided to answer. Caller ID said it was the ADA's cell.

"Hello, Nickie," Miranda said. "Have you found him?"

Nickie wouldn't mention the fact that she hadn't been looking for him but for evidence damning him. "I'm afraid not." Keep it casual, Nick. "I did come across something, however. Can you meet me in Captain Nolan's office in five?"

"What kind of something?"

"I'd really rather not explain over the phone. Dave knows I'm coming and that I requested your presence." Pause. Not the good kind either. "We're…I'm pulling into the station lot as we speak. Meet me?"

"Okay. I'm still searching Eddy's office. Stop by on your way, and I'll join you."

Nickie hung up and slid her hand beneath Duncan's as it rested on her leg. "She didn't mention my correction between we're and I'm."

Duncan nodded and lifted his hand so he could downshift. Damned manual transmission. "Or the fact that you said, 'Requested your presence.'"

He was right. That was too obvious. Her lids closed, and she sighed. It was time to get her head on straight. That skill seemed to slip away more each day.

He was opening her door before she had a chance to put those thoughts together. She grabbed the plastic bag with Eddy's confiscated laptop, swung her boots to the gravel and stood tall. "This won't beat me." She started to explain that she meant the news about her father…the revelation about Eddy.

"I know," he said and rested his warm lips on her forehead. Why did that mean so much more than a cheek or a hand, and why so different from the lips? She didn't care and decided to accept the gesture.

They walked hand-in-hand on the way to the stairwell. She was breaking all kinds of rules that day.

The climb to the fourth floor provided a pleasant burn in her thighs and pumped needed oxygen to her brain. One thing at a time. Her partner. Her father. Jun Zheng. In that order, damn it.

As they reached the top of the stairwell, Duncan released her hand and pushed open the door for her. In his other hand was his briefcase. Words weren't necessary at this point in their relationship. Not here. Not for this.

He paused and guided her in front of him, then cupped her elbow as they walked. Just one person looked up when she entered. Lucinda stuck a pencil behind her ear as Nickie passed. "Do you know how many phone calls we've gotten from the hospital since you left there?"

"No, why don't you tell me?" Nickie said without any hint of sarcasm.

Lucinda sat speechless. "Oh. A lot…I guess."

Duncan removed his hand from her elbow and turned into her office. She marched forward without stopping, pausing only for a moment at Eddy's door. The ADA sat at his desk. Officer Parker was there, a single hip resting on the corner. It was sweet. Parker's position on Eddy's desk was nearly in her lap. He sat twisting her ponytail. And Nickie thought she had crossed a line by holding hands with her husband in the stairwell?

She caught Miranda's gaze long enough to nod toward Dave's office.

Nickie knocked on the already open door just below the nameplate that read: Captain Dave Nolan.

"Thank you," Dave said into his phone as he waved them in before setting it face down on his desk. Nickie took one of his leather guest chairs. Miranda the other. Nickie rested the laptop on her legs.

"Any sign of him?" Dave squinted over his desk at the plastic evidence bag on her lap.

First things first. "I'm afraid not," she answered. "Except for the mold growing on the dirty dishes in the sink and on the counters, his apartment looks like he left for work this morning. No train or airline tickets or receipts that we could find. There are empty suitcases in his closet."

"We?" Miranda interrupted.

"Yes," Nickie said. "We had our phones turned off during the search, and Duncan called Dave as to my whereabouts. Scared the hell out of me when he showed." It wasn't a lie.

"I didn't find anything either," Miranda continued. "The desk in his office has a greasy paper towel on it with two leftover donuts that are quite old. There are two half-written reports from the cases he worked on before he was—" She swallowed hard before choking out the last word, "—shot."

Dave opened his mouth, but Nickie held up a finger. "There's more, I'm afraid." This was where she needed to be careful. The evidence she found on the laptop had to go on the books as an accidental find. "I need to backtrack to a few weeks ago. Duncan and I were searching for evidence of Jun Zheng's whereabouts. We inadvertently came across some emails." Was this where she inserted the careful? "Now, just hear me out," she said, holding up her hands, palms facing forward. "It isn't like I was trying to keep anything from you. It's just that it doesn't have anything to do with…" Nickie paused and shook her head at the inevitable fact that, yep, this was not going to end well.

Dave waited patiently. She would have preferred that he chided, interrupted or badgered her. Not wanting to witness the pain on Dave's face, she took a deep breath and squeezed her eyes shut. "While searching for information leading to the arrest and conviction of Jun Zheng, Duncan and I discovered—" It was her turn to swallow hard. "—emails from within a station account that have been sent to a covert outside source."

It was like a canker sore in the back of her mouth. She knew if she touched it with her tongue, it would hurt. Yet, she would touch it with her tongue anyway. She opened her eyes and saw Dave's expression. It was indeed a mixture of hurt, disappointment and several shades of red all changing before her eyes. Hurry up and get this over with, Nick. "Emails regarding me." Closing her eyes again, she let her chin dip in defeat.

"Wait a minute," Miranda interrupted. "Emails? How did you get into…?" She rubbed her fingers in circles around her temples. "I feel as if I need to remind you about evidence that is not admissible in…No."

Nickie's eyes opened, and she pulled her chin back.

"I realize," Miranda lectured. "That you have this super power regarding solid evidence that withstands court scrutiny, but…never mind. Trusting you now. Continue."

Nickie wished she could trust Miranda. The ADA was most likely on the up and up, but there had been too many players gone bad in her life to trust anyone. "The emails are in regards to me personally and my work on the Jun Zheng case."

She inhaled, ready to continue her pithy explanation, but there was no time for that. Dave roared as he cleared the contents of his desk in one quick swipe of his enormous arm. Miranda stood so fast she toppled her chair sideways onto the floor. Moving nothing except her eyes, Nickie glanced to Miranda, who stood with both hands covering her mouth.

"In my house," Dave yelled as he chucked the coffee mug he'd grabbed when wiping his desk clean. It shattered against a side wall of cabinets. "And you didn't tell me? This is my house," he repeated and pointed a finger to his chest. He growled as he circled the perimeter of his desk.

"These were emails about me. Not the department."

He stopped and stared at her with eyes that were glossing over with pain.

"Okay, okay, okay." She shook her head. "Jun Zheng is a department case." Sort of. "You're right. I don't play well with others. All right? I don't share. I'm not even a nice person."

"Keep going," he said.

"Dave, it was Eddy."

It took a minute to sink in. She knew when it hit him. The muscles in his face seemed to collapse. "Detective Lynx?"

She nodded. "I searched his apartment for evidence of his whereabouts." She glanced over to Miranda, who still stood in front of her toppled chair. "All of us were worried about him." Nickie only partially lied. "As I searched his apartment for him or anything that might tell me where he is, I found a laptop. Duncan and I hacked into it, hoping to find some kind of credit card activity, or email that may lead to his whereabouts. You know, the regular stuff. But, what we found was that the laptop is at least one of the machines used to send emails to the outside source."

She remained motionless as Miranda righted her chair and sat down. Dave sank into his chair as well.

"I'm afraid it's all starting to make sense," Nickie continued. "Eddy took Jun Zheng out of his cell for questioning without backup. Both Eddy and Phil the barber were shot with the same gun. Eddy's gun. One lives, one lays in a drawer in the morgue in the basement. Did Eddy move over to the dark side? He wouldn't be the first. Did he let Jun Zheng have his gun? Maybe he didn't know he would end up shot if he did. Regardless, he sent the emails, Jun Zheng is free, and Eddy sent his guard and me on a wild goose chase so that he could sneak out of the hospital."

Dave lifted his chin and leaned on his elbows. "This is my house," he growled once more. "You ever keep anything from me like this again, and I'll suspend you without pay."

He was serious. "Fair enough."

"And furthermore," he continued. "I'm taking you off all other cases. I want Lynx found and brought in for questioning. I want copies of all emails you and Duncan discovered. And what the hell is Duncan doing in your office while we're talking about him? Get him in here. I want to know everything."

Nickie sank lower in her chair, trying not to look at Miranda. "I…um. Dave, it's all sort of…"

Miranda stood and straightened her skirt. "I understand. You don't want to say anything in front of me. Frankly, I don't blame you. If I had been betrayed by my partner of several years, I would certainly not trust the relatively new assistant district attorney. However, the next time you want to search an apartment for evidence of wrongdoing without a warrant, put the facts on the table. I'm not stupid, Detective. And, I'm also not above leaving out facts that don't help our case. My professional opinion remains the same. Detective Lynx was under the residual effect of prescribed narcotics when he walked out of the hospital. Regardless of the intent, he is a missing detective under the influence. The search was legal. Don't treat me like an idiot again."

Wow. "You have my word." She meant it.

Duncan sat at Nickie's desk. Dim light came from the lamp at the corner and the glow from his tablet. Ignoring the whispers from the desk clerks and beat officers who resided in the commons area, he searched for pieces of Lynx's past. Why had he never considered Lynx? He chastised himself as the noise from Captain Nolan's office became louder.

Lynx had always been a loner. No family, no friends. Had he played Duncan that easily? Had he recognized Duncan's mixture of jealousy and protective nature for his Nickie?

"Okay, okay, okay," he heard Nickie yell as clearly as if she were standing next to him. "I don't play well with others. I don't share. I'm not even nice."

Dave's voice wasn't nearly as easy to understand, but made up for clarity in volume. "And what the hell is Duncan doing in your office while we talk about things that pertain to him?"

Recognizing the inevitable, Duncan logged out and closed applications on his tablet. "It's only a matter of time, Eddy Lynx," Duncan mumbled. "I owe you."

It took little time for the sound of two sets of purposeful female heels to come clicking toward Nickie's office. The first was the ADA. She broke off toward the elevator. Officer Parker had been leaning against the wall next to it ever since the meeting began.

Nickie came next and turned into her office. "I have bad news," she said.

"It's not like any of us didn't hear," Lucinda said, raising her voice from behind Nickie's back.

Nickie spun on her heels. As her back was to him, Duncan wasn't privy to the expression on his detective's face, but he had never seen Lucinda frightened before that moment, so it must have made an impact.

"The captain would like you to join us," Nickie said as she turned back to him.

"So I heard." They marched without speaking through the absolute silence of the commons area. As they entered Dave's office, Duncan spotted a small pond of yellow Post-it notes, pencil cups, a stapler, a cell and a few dozen papers strewn on the floor beside the far side of his desk.

Duncan sat in the farthest guest chair, stuck one leg straight out in front of him, then crossed the other at the ankle.

Nickie lowered into another chair and sat ramrod straight with her hands folded in her lap.

"I want answers," Dave said, still out of breath as he shut his office door. He howled once more about this being his house and of his distaste in being kept in the dark. Nickie, as well, repeated her excuses that included playing poorly with others, and a reluctance to share.

Duncan uncrossed his ankles and stood. The two of them all but ignored him as he walked to the back of the room. There stood a wall that held the old school, traditional dry erase boards that slid one over the other. One by one, he slid them until he found one that was clean.

Dave and Nickie were silent by this time. Finally. Duncan wasn't sure how much more he could have tolerated. He pulled the blank board all the way to the forefront, chose a marker and wrote.

Age 14. Abducted at gunpoint by Jun Zheng from her bedroom into Fu Haizi's trafficking ring. No signs of forced entry.

Age 15. Escaped captivity. Parents reluctant to her homecoming, portraying her as a spoiled runaway.

Age 18. Changed name from Nicole Monticello to Nickie Savage, mocking the nickname Jun Zheng had given her while in captivity.

Once he got into it, it was as if he couldn't stop himself. The information escaped from the confines of his eidetic memory, out his fingers and onto the board. The sensation of freedom made him write faster and faster. He created a complicated flow chart, including the times Nickie had been relocated over the last seventeen years through foster homes, then by crooked politicians and law enforcement all the way up to the dirty FBI special agents, each of which likely worked for Fu Haizi.

He hadn't finished when she took the marker from his hand and stood in front of it all. Looking at it in this form—the names and dates, the length, the number of betrayals—trapped him in a new abyss.

He glanced back and noticed Dave, leaning his backside against his empty desk, arms crossed and eyes red and swollen.

It must have been only a few moments, yet seemed like hours. She drew a long line from the top of the board to the bottom. In the separated white space, she wrote four things.

No signs of forced entry.

Records of abduction hidden by IEM employee.

Lynx hired to spy and report to same IEM employee.

IEM employee found murdered.

Dave appeared as if he'd just witnessed an entire platoon of friends killed in war. Duncan knew what that looked like. "What. Is. IEM?" The words dragged out of Dave's mouth like molasses.

"Import and Export Services," Duncan answered.

"Ivanna and Edward Monticello," Nickie interrupted, then dug into the inside pocket of her brown leather jacket, unfolding the printed picture within. "It's time to visit Daddy," she said and used a spare magnet to stick the photo of Jun Zheng and Edward Monticello next to her list.

"My house," Dave said once more. "Jun Zheng. Edward Monticello. It's all the same. You're a daughter to me, and I'm going with you."

CHAPTER 6

"Are you sure you're up for this?" Duncan asked.

She nodded and grinned.

"How can you possibly smile at a time like this?" he said.

Her chest expanded, then released in a whoosh. "I know. It's calloused."

He reached for her hand and laced his warm fingers in hers. "That was not my intent. I meant how do you remain positive in the midst of loose ends and deceit?"

They rode to Duncan's aunt and uncle's home for Saturday morning scones with all the windows rolled down. Nickie held her hair in her right hand to keep it from blowing all over the place. The air was clear. The sky was blue and the temperature a perfect seventy-five degrees.

Xena rode in the back with her head sticking out the window. Nickie supposed all dogs did that, but this was her dog, and since she'd never had one before, it made her smile. She loved the way Xena's lips and ears flapped in the wind each time Duncan reached thirty miles an hour. She kept sniffing the air, then sneezing from sniffing the air.

"I can smile, because I'm calloused. My motto? Laugh or cry. It's kept me alive so far."

"You've risked your life for dozens, possibly hundreds of victims. You take the time to arrange counseling for the children." He squeezed her fingers. "And you smile in the midst of betrayal and life-shattering news because a dog is happy. You are far from calloused." Lifting their joined hands, he kissed the backs of her knuckles one at a time before resting his lips on her wedding ring.

"As a child, I was forced to sell myself or be beaten. My father's involvement in my abduction? My partner stabbing me in the back? It sucks, don't get me wrong, but it's nothing compared to what the girls I left behind endured."

The muscles in his jaw flexed and released.

He bumped over the Black Creek bridge, and Xena stood in the backseat. She whined and circled, then whined more. "She knows," Nickie said. "How does she always know?"

Mature oaks and maples grew in natural clusters on both sides of the Reed drive. The leaves were a deep green, reminding Nickie that spring had slipped by and somehow changed into summer. Duncan turned up the sloped drive and stopped. "Brie would graciously understand if we missed Saturday morning scones. I know you're anxious to dig into Lynx's laptop."

Now, that really made her smile. "What laptop?"

"The one I saw you walk out with after our meeting with Dave."

"Meeting? Is that what you call it? More like an adult tantrum by a large, grown man."

"Justified tantrum."

"Okay, okay. And Brie would understand. My foster mother, on the other hand, would not be gracious or understanding if I missed supper tomorrow evening." She shrugged. "If we're doing one, we're doing the other."

Xena's whines turned into more of a howl. Nickie pointed her thumb over her shoulder and toward the backseat. "And try and tell that one we're turning around and going home. My father isn't going anywhere. It will do me good to take time and get away from it." She smiled from ear to ear now. "And the laptop."

"You will share the location of this confiscated piece of equipment? I have a brother who would like to get his hands on it."

"I may possibly also have in my possession one confiscated monitor and tower from said fugitive."

"You stole Lynx's work computer?"

"Borrowed."

"You took evidence from a police department."

"Tomato to-mah-to." Nickie spotted her right away. Duncan's aunt wore youthful blue jeans and a slate blue, short-sleeved flannel shirt. Her kneepads were bright pink and matched the gardening gloves she wore as she trimmed something fuzzy and bushy.

Duncan's uncle came from the garage carrying a bag of mulch over his shoulder. He wouldn't call these people aunt or uncle or even Brie and Nathan. These were his parents, more so than Nickie's birth parents ever were for her.

The muscles in Duncan's entire body seemed to release as he spotted them, a stark reminder of how much life with her was riddled with stress. The sight of his brother's Jeep lifted Nickie's spirits. Andy and Rose were the only friends she had.

"This may be a working breakfast," Duncan said as Andy came out shortly after Nathan with a bag on each shoulder. Rose followed with Andy Jr. in her arms.

In the backseat, Xena was beyond reason.

"You better stop here. She's going to put scratches on your door."

He stopped and Nickie reached behind her, dodging paws and pulled the door handle next to Xena. She took off out the door and ran full force toward the house. But it wasn't Nathan or Brie she was after. The Reed golden retriever bound down the drive as fast as Xena. You would think they hadn't just seen each other last Saturday by the jumping and yelping, rolling and whining. Yes. She could smile at a time like this.

"Hey, Nick," Rose said as she met them at Duncan's car. "I would have brought the infant backpack if I'd known there was yard work this morning. How goes it?"

Nickie nodded, then lied. "Good. Really good. You?"

"Work is great. A.J. is getting faster every day." Except, then she squinted at her. "You haven't been by to see your horse lately."

Or Rose for that matter. And it wasn't technically Nickie's horse. She was just the only one Abigail allowed on her back these days.

"She gets cranky when you haven't been by, and she doesn't play well with others when she gets cranky."

Duncan came around and met them at the front of his car. "She's my horse, and she's not the only one who doesn't play well with others."

"Yo," Andy said as he hefted two of the bags to the spot Brie pointed at before walking toward them. "I've been working on something." He looked over his shoulder toward Nathan and Brie.

It was obvious Andy had some secret, something he wanted to spill. Nickie should have been interested. It clearly had something to do with her. She heard a few words. Dummy trail. Maps. Locations.

Except Nickie was too mesmerized with Brie. She used long-handled trimmers to cut off mutant branches that grew like bad hair from the bulk of one of the fuzzy bush things. That was what Nickie was doing with Fu Haizi. She was taking down one branch at a time. Saving a single group of children was good. It was rewarding and important. But she needed to turn her focus to the trunk. Or was that a stem? The roots?

She shook her head. It didn't matter. She was so focused on saving branches of children, she hadn't been thinking about the big picture. Where were the headquarters? Did Jun Zheng have a headquarters? What about records, names, locations?

"Nick?"

"Let her go," Duncan answered Rose. "She's onto something, I can tell."

"Huh?" Nickie asked, looking around and realizing the five of them all stood staring at her.

"What do you think, Nick?" Rose asked.

"I think I'm anxious to get out and ride Abigail."

Duncan brought Xena with him. He had to wake her from her training crate, but she would have known Duncan was out of bed and downstairs and eventually woken Nickie with her whimpers.

Sleep remained a rare luxury for his Nickie and something that would evade Duncan as well until the day Jun Zheng was back in police custody and Fu Haizi dismantled. The only light in the room came from the lamp setting an arm's length away and the glow from the tablet he wasn't using. It caused him to ponder the last time he sat at a desk in the dark, a few short days ago in Nickie's office.

Lucinda, the clerk who sat on the other side of Nickie's door, had come in as he searched for background on Eddy Lynx. She pretended her purpose was to obtain his signature on a copy of the local magazine edition covering his upcoming art show. Duncan saw through her performance. She had mostly been fishing for a reason behind the tongue lashing her mentor and idol, Detective Savage, was currently enduring in Captain Nolan's office.

Xena lifted her snout from its resting spot on her front feet and sniffed the air. Placing his hand on her head, he scratched between her eyes until she set her enormous head back on her paws. Her eyes remained alert, scanning the room Duncan had chosen for his middle-of-the-night work. Why had he chosen his gunroom? He wasn't sure. Glass cabinets. Hidden cabinets. Legally reported firearms.

For the time being, Duncan focused on the paper files he'd stolen from Leslie Jacobsen's office weeks prior. Leslie Jacobsen. The recipient of the surveillance emails Eddy Lynx had been secretly sending from the station. Leslie Jacobsen who had undoubtedly worked for Jun Zheng. And who now laid six feet under.

He stopped to rub his eyes with his thumb and forefinger. It wasn't the first time he'd combed through the files, but he hoped to find something he may have missed. Although they seemed legitimate, he sensed something that brought several of them together. A common thread he couldn't quite connect. The one he concentrated on was labeled Mariposa Joven. Young butterfly. It mentioned some kind of drop box for files pertaining to importing and exporting materials used to create earth-moving equipment. Metamorphosis, he assumed. Taking the materials and creating something new with them? Where was this drop box? What files?

Pushing away from the papers, he stared at the screen and ground his teeth. He reached down to provide a few more scratches to Xena's forehead. It caused her to purr much like a cat.

Closing his eyes, he decided to ponder the large map his brother had mentioned that morning at their aunt's home. Andy explained that he'd taken a magic marker and made dots for each dummy location Eddy Lynx's IP addresses had traveled through. The false trail was a system similar to what Andy used when he and Duncan hacked into secure databases. Send the signal through several locations, in country and out. If they were ever detected, by the time the suspecting receiver traced through half the fabricated locales, Duncan and Andy would be long gone. Although Andy had adapted their methods as technology morphed over the years, the basic system served them well.

Now, the method had been used against his detective. But what did this mean?

Duncan's phone buzzed. It was two a.m. "Speak of the devil. I was just thinking about your IP address map."

"Have you been outside?" Andy asked.

Reflexively, Duncan's eyes turned to the window. It was coal black that evening. A haze blocked out the stars and the moon was on the other side of the world.

"Why do you ask?" With Andy living just down the road, it was a valid question.

"I thought I saw someone walking around up there. A few someones actually."

At that moment, Xena's purr turned into a growl that likely only Duncan and Nickie could differentiate.

"Did Xena just growl?"

Or maybe Andy as well.

Fire raced through his veins. "I'll call you ba—"

"I'm coming up."

"Don't be an idiot. I'm locked up and safe inside. You wouldn't be."

"You're my brother. I already came close to losing you once in my life—"

Duncan didn't have the time or the patience for this. "How about if you don't hear from me in ten, you can call the police."

"Don't you sleep with a cop?"

Xena growled harder this time. Clicking off the desk lamp, Duncan whispered into the phone, "Calling you back in ten." He hung up his cell. By memory, he opened his gun cabinet in the dark and felt for his Remington 870. A shotgun was overkill, but Duncan was done with this shit.

His senses on overdrive, he crept through the black halls on the balls of his feet. Xena heeled next to his left leg. She walked as softly as he did. His eyes adjusted to the dark by the time he reached the main floor.

With his back flat against each wall, he maneuvered from room to room until he reached the back of the house. Large shadows ducked from tree to tree. Going in low, he cracked open one of the glass French doors that led from the kitchen out back. He dropped to the deck boards and pointed the shotgun using his shoulder to steady his aim. Xena crawled on her belly and lay next to him. They were silent, like his platoon waiting for insurgents to make their move.

Squinting his left eye, his right watched through the scope of the gun, darting from one tree trunk to another. Wait on it. Wait on it. The heat made the powdery sand stick to each crevice in his body and covered his clothing.

Hot wind whipped the loose end of the strap on his pack as it weighed him down and pressed his body into the desert sand. A flash of light caused him to blink several times. He couldn't hear anything. Was it the explosion they had all been waiting for?

Several lanky men darted from behind pillars of ancient stones. One of the stray dogs that followed them everywhere took off after them. He pulled back on the pump of his Remington, cocking the gun to shoot to kill before being shot and killed.

"Duncan!" It was a female voice. Equality be damned. He never could get used to having women in the line of this kind of fire.

"It's okay. See? It's me."

The voice was familiar. It could be a trick. He shook his head and blinked.

"It was a pack of deer, Duncan. See? It's me, Nickie." Then, she turned on the outside spotlights.

"Deer? In the desert?" His eyes clamped shut as he tried to process. "Nickie." Oh no. He opened his trembling fingers and let the shotgun drop to the floor. He hadn't even engaged the safety. Instinct fought him, but he forced his body to turn and face her. She grabbed a hand towel as she tiptoed toward him.

Squatting dangerously near his stiff body, she wiped the sweat from his brow. "Poor thing. What is this all about, anyway? You don't have…episodes…randomly. Did Xena alert you?"

Andy's call. The dark. Yes, Xena. "I'm tired," he answered.

"Of course you are. It's three a.m. I'm here."

"Andy called. I saw something." He shook his head. "Or I may have seen something and overreacted. Xena?"

She nodded and sat down beside him, drawing her knees up and resting her forearms on top of them. "Deer. A half dozen of them at least. They ran when I flipped on the light. Or maybe because Xena took off after them."

"They aren't getting better," he said, referring to his flashbacks. She would understand.

"Yes, they are. Baby steps."

The distinct sound of four paws plodding through the moist leaves of the forest came from behind their home. The scent of mud and foliage blew the irrational from his mind. Xena had found something out there and held it in her mouth as she padded up the deck stairs. Duncan hoped it wasn't alive. He was suddenly tired, his arms and legs becoming lethargic and his body damp with cold sweat. He'd dealt with enough death that evening, even if most of it was in memory only.

"Duncan," Nickie alerted. "Look."

He moved his gaze to the contents in Xena's teeth. She wagged her tail as she gripped a black glove she'd found. Lifting his brows, he looked to Nickie who looked back with the same conclusion written on her face.

CHAPTER 7

Nickie checked messages on her phone as Duncan parked in the front spot by the mailbox. It was the first time she could remember arriving at her childhood foster home on a Sunday afternoon early enough to get the spot closest to the drive.

"We don't have to stay," Duncan said as he turned off the Jaguar and pulled the emergency brake.

He'd said that at the end of the drive at his folks' place, too. "No. It's the right thing to do." She lifted her chin from her phone and glanced over to the only house of the many houses she'd lived in as a child that she considered home. It was the same as it always was. Small, simple, manicured. She liked that. "The pots are out and have flowers in them."

"It is June," he said as he opened his car door.

June. When did that happen? Yes, she was quite sure she was up for this today. Time with people who positively weren't going to stab her in the back? Yes, please.

No messages about anything department mole or Fu Haizi related. Trip to interrogate her father scheduled for the morning. "Yes," she said. "This is the right thing to do." Stuffing her phone in her pocket, she picked up the pan of the only appetizer thing she knew how to make. As she stepped out, warm sun poured over her.

She glanced to his face but stopped short when she noticed his expression. "You're scowling."

The chocolate brown of his eyes turned to meet hers. "Did you say, 'scowling'?"

"I did. You are." She slipped her free hand into his. "I have people."

He lifted a single brow. "You've mentioned that once or twice."

"People I can trust. My foster family."

He gently squeezed her fingers.

"And your family."

His grip tightened.

"I have my captain." This time he slid his arm behind her. She stepped in and pressed her body into his. "And I have you."

His chin turned away, but his glance stayed with her.

"What?" she asked.

"I'm waiting for the rest."

Turning toward the house, she wrapped her arm around him. "Sheesh. What more do you need?"

"The part where if I repeat any of that, you'll kick my ass."

Damn it if a traitorous smile didn't spread over her face. "Well, there is that." Juggling the pan and her swelling heart, she glanced up and noticed her foster mother watching them through the screen of the storm door. Gloria smiled before turning to head back into the house.

"See?" Nickie chided. "Now you have Gloria all curious and confused."

The smell of warm bread and spicy sauce filled her head and helped her know that she was home. The house was the same. Always the same. She liked that, too. The carpet may be threadbare, but not a crumb could be found anywhere. Mismatched furniture, organized and cozy. It was the kind of place where a guest was welcome to leave their shoes on but took them off anyway. She led Duncan to the kitchen where she would find Gloria.

Standing at the stove, her foster mother scraped what smelled like sautéed onions, garlic and celery into a giant pot of marinara sauce. Gloria's marinara sauce. Score.

"You are early," Gloria said as she placed the lid on the monstrous pot.

"I brought—"

"Stromboli," Gloria finished for her. "I was counting on it." She turned and dried her hands on her apron. Her smile was slight, yet brightened her entire face. Gloria tilted her head from one side to another. "You look healthy, my child." Nickie walked to her and rested her cheek on Gloria's shoulder as her hefty arms wrapped around Nickie's back. This was one of the few female embraces Nickie could understand.

Gloria pulled away and turned to Duncan. Her smile dropped almost instantly. She stepped to him and placed her hands on his cheeks. "You are scowling."

Nickie would have snorted if she knew how. Without responding, Duncan glanced to Nickie before turning back to Gloria.

"Set the table," Gloria said. "We have a full house coming today." As if she ever didn't have a full house.

Nickie and Duncan set out plates at the long dining table as well as the small worn one in the center of the kitchen and the one in the nook. Even so, there would be people eating on couches with plates on their laps. A few dozen napkins and sets of silverware later and the front door began to open and bang shut.

Salt and peppershakers, napkin holders for each table. Duncan lifted his head, then turned for the front door. Nickie had enough time to place pepper jam and crackers at each table before he returned. Great-Grandmama was on his arm. Had he heard her car? Sometimes Nickie thought his eidetic memory worked as supersonic hearing, too.

"I've got twenty bucks that says my zombies beat your zombies." The teenage words coming from Great-Grandmama's mouth made Nickie scrunch her face like she'd just eaten lime after a shot of tequila.

"You're on, old woman," Duncan said as he hung her jacket on the coat stand.

Using her cane, she shuffled out of the way of the sound of small feet smacking the concrete walk. The door flew open and Gil's twin daughters blew through like the wind. Did Great-Grandmama have supersonic hearing, too? Gil and Teresa followed a few steps behind with their twin infant sons' carriers in hand.

"Mista Weed!" little Nala yelled. "I told you that was Mista Weed's car," she said to her sister. Lela wrapped herself around one of his thighs and Nala around the other. He reached down and picked them up, one in each arm. "I found cookies," he told them. They squealed at the news and squirmed enough that he almost dropped them. "Whoa. I don't think you can have any ye—"

They hit the floor and ran for the kitchen anyway. "Ha," she said in a whisper. "And you want kids. We can't even keep them from cookies before supper."

The scowl came back in full force. He sighed and repeated in an equally low, yet scowly, tone. "The timeliness of cookie-eating has little to do with acceptable parenting."

The sound of animated gunshots came from the next room, distracting her from the direction of their conversation. She looked around. The people she loved. The ones who loved her back. Unconditionally. Regardless of her past. Or her present.

She took Duncan's hand and marched for the kitchen.

"Not until after dinner," Gloria said to the twins as Nickie stepped in.

"Gloria, I…um. Hey, don't answer any phone calls from my partner, Detective Lynx. Okay? Just for a while. Well, or from my mother or father. I'll let you know when all is well again."

There was a short pause before Gloria turned back to her cutting board and sliced more pieces of bread to go with supper.

"Or any from a Maryland number in general," Nickie added. "You will see the origin of the phone call on your cell phone." Nickie pulled hers out. "See? You can tell right here."

No pause this time or even a glance to see what Nickie was pointing to.

"I know how to see where phone call comes from." Her Latina accent became pronounced when she was agitated.

"I'm not trying to scare you, it's just that—"

This time, Gloria turned to face her and squared her shoulders. "I've been kidnapped and threatened by this Jun Zheng. Now, I need to beware of the people who abandoned you? You are my daughter!" Gloria rarely raised her voice, and it scared Nickie more this time than any other. Gloria had indeed been kidnapped. For Nickie's sake. To scare and manipulate Nickie. And it had worked.

"Yes," Nickie said and held up her arms in surrender. "Which is why I'd really like for you to ignore any contact from them. Call me right away if it happens."

"What is this? Why?" Gloria stopped, closed her eyes and took a deep breath. "You tell me what is happening. You are my daughter," she repeated. "I deserve to know."

"We all do." It was Gil's voice. Nickie turned to see him and Teresa standing in the doorway, arms crossed. She didn't want to go there. It was too dangerous.

"They deserve to know." Duncan. The four of them stood in a line like Nickie was in an intervention. The twins scurried under their arms and out the kitchen door, the miniature traitors.

"I don't know anything for sure," Nickie said.

"Bullshit," Gil said. Gloria didn't even reprimand him for using language in her home.

No one bothered to look to Duncan for answers. It was like being thrown under a bus with an engine Nickie had started. "I wasn't prepared for this today." She paced, trying to decide the best way to limit what she should say while still saying what needed to be said to keep her family safe.

"And don't hold back thinking you are keeping us safe," Teresa said like she'd read Nickie's mind.

Her feet paused their pacing before continuing. "It looks like Detective Lynx is working for my father."

Several undecipherable Spanish words came from Gil. Nickie kept her gaze on the floor, not willing to risk eye contact with any of them. "And my father is working for Jun Zheng." See? Simple. She breathed easier and turned to face them. "So, I'm going to confront my father. I just need you to stay away from your phones for a while. Oh, and maybe check the door before you answer."

She looked from one set of eyes to another. Uh oh. Duncan was the only one not staring at her. His eyes were closed and his head swayed back in forth in disbelief.

Gil growled so low she could hardly heard him. "We're going with you."

"Wait a minute." She held up her hand. "You can't—" This was worse than with her captain.

"Yes, we can," Gloria said in her frustrated and unbendable voice.

Teresa crossed her arms tighter and expanded her rib cage.

"Duncan?" Help?

"It's really not a good idea," he answered. Finally, a voice of reason. "We don't want to alert him or bring additional attention to you or your families."

"Psssst," Gloria hissed. "Kidnapped? Held in warehouse. Me."

"Yes," Duncan agreed in his smoothest voice. "And something we can't ever allow to happen again. I'll go with her."

Gloria tapped her foot for longer than Nickie's patience preferred. "Do we have your word?"

"Yes, of course," Duncan said. "And we will report our findings back to each of you. We're sorry for the danger you've been—"

"Stop," Gloria barked. "My daughter. Jun Zheng is involved with all. I feel it," she said as she pointed to her heart. "Here. He took me." She moved her finger away from her chest and toward Nickie. "To get to you. And this Edward and Ivanna who abandoned you?" She pretended to spit on the floor.

"Okay, okay," Nickie said. "I didn't mean to cause trouble at your beautiful Sunday supper. I will come back as soon as I know anything. I promise. Please. Let's eat."

Other than the sound of flatware clinking the table settings, dinner was silent. Lead weights pulled Nickie's shoulders forward. With big eyes, the children peered from one adult to another as they ate.

"When is the next ball game?" Duncan asked Lela and Nala as plates emptied in the quiet. The two of them checked the expressions of the other adults, then shrugged in unison and turned to their mother, who pulled one of the infant twins from his carrier.

"Friday night," Teresa said in a short, curt voice. "Six o'clock." She rose from the table and bounced the baby. "That's his tired cry," Teresa said as if she was somehow only talking to Nickie. "Here," Teresa said as she held the crying baby out toward her.

Nickie looked from Teresa to the baby to Duncan. This was her punishment for ruining Sunday lunch? Pins and needles covered her body. She'd rather pull an all-night stakeout in front of Get Lucky's.

Just as Teresa began to deposit the wailing baby into her arms, Nickie turned to Duncan again. He had the nerve to grin. It was his evil grin. She tried to say something but nothing came out, so she lifted her arms before it fell to the ground. What about its head? Which arm should she use? Nickie sighed and took him, still not knowing which twin he was. She stood, walked and attempted to do the bounce thing she saw Teresa do.

Taking her punishment like a man, she bounced her way into the video game room. The baby stiffened and dug his face into Nickie's boob. No, no, no. She looked around for help, but the teenagers ignored her and the baby. Couldn't they hear him? The cries became quieter. Worried, she looked down at him. Long blinks were followed by tiny fists that rubbed his eyes.

Teresa knew. Of course she did. She was a good mom. The little guy rubbed his hands across his face and soon fell asleep with his mouth formed in a small O. It was the sweetest damned frigging thing she'd ever seen. As if she carried a three-tiered wedding cake, she sank into the side of the couch. Was this Jorge? Rico? It didn't matter as long as he stayed sleeping.

Dishes clinked and soon the busy talking that came with these suppers returned. Paranoia scratched the surface of Nickie's mind. Had they tried to get her out of the room on purpose? It was rare that she felt alienated in this home, yet there it was. At least the baby smelled good. Were they supposed to smell good? Nothing made sense anymore.

The telltale sound of Great-Grandmama's cane entered the room. Oh no. Nickie had chosen the video game room to put a baby to sleep? She knew she wasn't right for this. Without moving her chin, she watched the little guy— which one was this again?—as Spanish-speaking teenaged cousins came in and sat with Great-Grandmama. Their talking didn't wake the baby. Or the rustling of the couch, or the noise of the television. Was he sick? Still alive? Surely, she couldn't kill off a baby by holding him, could she?

Nala and Lela came in, each with chocolate stuck to the corners of their mouths. Nala sat with Great-Grandmama as she killed zombies with a crossbow. This alternate world was confusing and not a little disconcerting. Lela slid next to Nickie and lay her head on Nickie's leg. As long as she was stuck here, she would lay her head back on the couch, too.

Teresa nudged her shoulder. "Nickie," she said. "Unless you're taking these two with you, I need to get home." Two? Nickie blinked and glanced around. The room was empty and quiet. She looked down to find baby Jorge, or was this Rico, sleeping on one side of her and Lela on the other.

"You have a family," Teresa said. "We are your family."

CHAPTER 8

Nickie sat at her desk in the station as she clicked on the printer icon. "Oh, shit," she said as she realized she'd tossed her coat on the machine. Almost toppling the bottle of water on her desk, she leaned over and grabbed it before everything jammed.

Off all other cases? Focus all of her energies on finding Eddy Lynx and taking down Fu Haizi? Was this good or bad?

Since the original copy of the press photo taken with Jun Zheng and her father remained stuck to her captain's old school dry erase board, she printed another to keep in her possession. In the photo, Zheng and her father weren't communicating or even facing each other. Anyone looking at it would assume the two men didn't know each other. However, there were unlikely coincidences and there were unfathomable coincidences. She didn't believe in either, and this fell into the latter category. As the printer grunted, she opened the top right drawer of her splintered desk.

Glaring at her was the business card from FBI Special Agent Hurst. Although written in pencil, his personal phone number stared at her as if it was written in neon orange.

He had taken the initiative to run the check on the department mole that was ratting out her every move. He'd offered.

She should call him. She needed to call him. It was the ethical thing to do. Integrity and all that.

If she knew for certain he wasn't siphoning information to Jun Zheng, she would call without hesitation. He'd helped her. Been on her side. If it weren't for him, she would still be hanging with backstabbing Eddy Lynx, solving cases as a team for the good of the world.

Hurst's predecessors had moved to the dark side. How did she know he hadn't done so, too? She grabbed the card, plopped it on her desk and dialed.

"Good morning, Detective Savage. I was just going to call you."

Another unbelievable coincidence. Nickie said, "I wanted to let you know that I recently discovered Detective Eddy Lynx is the department mole. I wouldn't have learned this without the intel you provided. Thank you."

"Yes. I have eyes out there keeping a watch for him. No sign of him thus far."

He did? Why?

"I had the hospital call me as soon as they woke him from the coma. They notified me, also, of his disappearance."

"Oh." He knew Eddy was in the hospital?

He must have recognized the confusion in her tone because he continued with, "He was the last person to see Jun Zheng before his escape from county."

She sighed, but tried not to let him hear it. He had not only given her the intel that led her to Eddy's guilt, Hurst had also allowed her to keep Jun Zheng in her custody when he was wanted for federal inquisition. Now, he was free.

"Well." She sounded stupid. "I just wanted to make sure you knew and to thank you for your help." Stupider.

"Everything okay, Detective?"

"Yes, of course. Always."

"Keep my card, Nick." His voice softened from his stiff special agent tone to his touch of unguarded speech. "I'm here for you, 'kay?"

"Yes. Um. Again, thank you."

Her suspicions weren't going away anytime soon, and she was scum for having them.

"Detective Dude!" The voice came from the commons area.

Her face winced like fingernails had raked over a chalkboard. Forcing her eyes to glance up, she spotted the nosy desk clerk, Lucinda, with her arm outstretched in front of Slippery Jimbo. He waved a hand around her like he and Nickie were long lost friends or something.

Great.

Nickie walked around her desk. Lucinda didn't even bother to look over her shoulder to see if Nickie was okay with him showing up. The nerve. "Hey, hey, hey," Nickie yelled at Lucinda as she left her office and entered the commons area.

Lucinda ignored her and took Jimbo's shoulders, attempting to turn him toward the elevator he'd come out of.

"You can't touch me, loser," Jimbo said to Lucinda. "I have rights."

Loser? "Hey, Slippery Jimbo, only I can call her a loser." Nickie took Lucinda's fingers and peeled them from Jimbo's shoulders. Lucinda fought her like it was okay to do that. "What the hell are you doing?" Nickie barked at her. "Let go of him, loser."

"You told me, and I quote, this man was to never, ever, ever, in his life enter this station, ever, ever, without your permission." Lucinda's snarky tone was more than Nickie could tolerate.

"Is this true, Detective Dude? I'm hurt, man. Really hurt."

"Permission," Nickie snapped and pulled Jimbo along by the sleeve of his nasty shirt. "My office. Move." She lowered her voice and added, "That shit grin is going to get your ass kicked, Jimbo. Get rid of it."

"Will do, Detective Dude. It's the least—" He turned his head and said as loud as he could. "—an informant can do for his detective, Detective Dude."

Pulling him along, she dragged him into her office and shut the door.

"What are you doing here?" Even though they entered the heat of the summer, his hair was greased back and he wore his knee-length light brown trench coat. "Hey, you got your cast off," she said, taking the edge from her snark. The broken arm he'd earned on her behalf. The sleeve of his coat did little to hide the skinny arm and peeling skin that came from wearing a cast for weeks. "Here," she added and took the stuff from one of her guest chairs and set it on the other. "Sit."

His eyes went right to the printer and picture of her father and Jun Zheng. She snatched it from the tray, then walked around her desk and stuffed it in the desk drawer.

"There's word out."

Eyeing him, she sank in her chair and contemplated. Less was more, so she waited him out.

He looked around at her office and her mess a little too long, but she was patient. "It's not that I saw anything personal," he said, still scanning her stuff.

"Personally," she corrected.

"What's personally?"

"You said personal. That's not right. It's personally."

"I said not personal. I ain't seen nothin' personal."

She rubbed her hands over her face, then along the top of her hair. "Okay, Jimbo. You have two minutes. Ready, go."

"Sheesh, man. Okay. People—"

"What peo—? Never mind. Continue."

"People," he enunciated, "have said they've seen Zheng around."

Her body stiffened at the idea that Zheng had been close, but she leaned back in her chair, slung one boot on her desk, then the other.

"Not me personal, but people. Ya know," he said as a statement.

"No, I don't know, Jimbo. Why don't you explain?"

Beads of sweat formed along his upper lip and his greasy hairline. "Around."

"Like Phil the barber's place around?"

"That place?" he asked and tapped his fingers on the armrests of her guest chair. "No, no. That place has been empty ever since Phil…" He used his forefinger to run a line from one side of his neck to the other.

"Where, then? When?"

"Get Lucky's. T & As." He shrugged and looked up and to his right. The sign of a lie. "The usual."

"You know this doesn't help me. Why are you telling me this? Why are you here?"

He looked around as if someone might be listening through the walls. "Zheng is a bad man, Detective Dude."

No shit.

"I want you to be on the lookout. Be safe, man. Keep your eyes open."

Keep your eyes open. That was what Phil the barber had said days before he was murdered. Murdered by Zheng, she was sure of it. Using Eddy Lynx's gun.

"So, how's the missing cop case?"

As if she would answer that. Interesting. "Speaking of, I have something for you to do since you've come to me with shit I can't use."

His eyes perked up like a kid in a candy store. Irritating. "Keep your eyes open for said missing cop. Maybe look around more than the usual spots. Ask around to your cryptic friends who seem to have spotted Zheng, yet remain nameless."

"Oh yeah, Detective Dude. I can do that. How much?"

"For a guy who's brought me zip, you don't get to ask me that. See what you can dig up, then we'll talk dollars."

Nickie sat next to Duncan in the passenger seat of his Jaguar. The windows were down, and the Maryland air was clean and fresh. Duncan found himself taking cleansing breaths for more reasons than the clean, fresh air.

"Pulling up to this house with you next to me is an entirely different experience," she said. Her demeanor was disconcertingly calm and collected. He could not say the same for himself.

It was apparent even from this distance that the home was enormous, ten thousand plus square feet at least. He wasn't sure if he could think of it as a home, although. Stone, not brick, with tall white pillars standing guard along the corners and adorning the front door. A museum would be more accurate, or possibly a prison.

He slowed his car to a stop in front of a ten-foot black, wrought iron fence. On the other side was a long drive that led to the residence.

Lining the drive were a few dozen evergreens that towered over twenty feet each in two straight rows like rigid soldiers. His expertise in the military was with explosives. With it came a trained eye. He spotted a number of cameras in the trees and along the fence. Shifting the Jag into neutral, he pulled the emergency brake so he could get out and ring the buzzer. Nickie took his hand and signaled for him to wait.

It took only a short moment, and the gate opened. They were being watched. He trolled up the smooth asphalt, approaching the narrow side that wound around the east of the home.

"Don't take that way," Nickie said, apparently reading his mind. "Go to the front." She pointed to a circle drive that surrounded a large fountain spraying water over a plethora of tiger lilies and lotus flowers.

"Are you sure?" The circle drive clearly was meant for show.

"When I come for a visit, I park with my side wheels on the first step." Her smile was as disconcerting as her demeanor and brought him back to scowling.

He parked and exited the vehicle, surprised that she paused long enough to allow him the time to walk around and assist with her car door. She stretched and yawned as she stood. In all the time they'd been together, he'd never seen her do this before. She was on stage. She was on stage and performing as such.

"Shall we?" she asked and tucked her arm in his.

They climbed the steps to the biggest door he'd ever seen. He painted for politicians and Oscar award-winning actresses. He'd seen big. A metallic lion glared at them from the center of the door, a circular knocker hanging from its teeth. Nickie rapped on the wood with her knuckles. "It's a formality," she mumbled. "They know we're here."

The door opened almost immediately. An older gentleman who looked as if he may have come straight out of a role as the butler in a 1930s movie answered the knock. Behind him was an enormous foyer surrounded by two symmetrically placed adjoining hallways. A flowing staircase led to a third-floor landing several dozen yards long that hovered like a cantilever.

"Detective Savage," the man said slowly before turning to Duncan. "Mr. Reed."

Transparency was overrated. Duncan had to dip his head in order to achieve eye contact with the man. He held out his hand. "Good day to you, sir. And your name is?"

The eye contact was short lived as the butler turned his gaze and answered. "My name is Clarence."

Brushing off the formalities, Nickie sniffed and asked, "Is he here?"

"Mr. Monticello is not available, Detective."

"He's not available, or he's not here?"

Without attempting to hide his disdain, the butler answered, "He is not here."

Imitating his tone and posture, Nickie retorted, "And when will he return?"

"Any moment now," he answered as if she hadn't just mocked him.

"Great. We'll take a walk down memory lane while we wait."

Her statement seemed to bewilder the butler. His back stiffened and he looked up to her as if she said she was planning a happy hour on the grounds. "You may wait in the front library, Detective."

"I grew up here, doc. I'm going to show my husband around. Don't worry your pretty little head. The cameras will be recording my every move, including your attempt to get me to stay put."

He didn't move out of the way, so Nickie stepped around him, pulling Duncan's arm as she did. She didn't get far. Her feet stopped and her neck craned from one side of the stone foyer floor to the other. As her eyes grew larger, her nails dug into the flesh of the bicep she held onto.

"This." Her voice shook as if the floor was opening beneath them.

Both Duncan and the butler followed her gaze to the floor. On it was an expansive stone creation spanning the length and width of the area. It was the largest stone artistry Duncan had ever seen. Grays, blacks and browns in different shades created an artistically embedded falcon.

CHAPTER 9

"This, this, this." Nickie began tapping at Duncan's chest as if she didn't already have his undivided attention. "It's the falcon from Phil the barber's forearm. It was a new tat. I saw it at the morgue."

He remembered the story.

She circled the entire area as if she didn't want to step on the rendering. "I knew I remembered it from somewhere." Her feet stopped again. This time she looked to Duncan. "Oh, Duncan." Her voice grew low. "We should have brought backup."

"Clarence?" A male voice came from the end of a long hallway. The click of designer shoes preceded it. "Clarence, do tell me who is raising their voice in our humble home?" Edward Monticello came into view sporting a designer coat and hat matching the color of his alligator skin shoes.

Ivanna followed behind. Other than the eyes and shape of Ivanna's mouth, Nickie's parents' appearances differed greatly from their daughter's. He'd forgotten how difficult it was for him to place them as blood relatives with his Nickie. The larger size of the high-end, conservative clothing was of little relevance. Each carried themselves with confidence and grace. The condescending expression said that Edward knew who was raising her voice in his *humble home*.

"Nicole, dear," Edward said, nearly squealing. "You've brought *the* Duncan Reed with you. Have we told you, Duncan, how pleased we are that our Nicole took her upbringing to heart in accepting the proposal of such an upstanding member of our social class?"

Yes, Edward had mentioned it before.

"We mean that as the highest of compliments, you understand," Edward said, closing his eyes and nodding.

Nickie stood in what Duncan thought of as her rock-star stance. Feet spread, knees locked.

Taking Edward's hand, Duncan made eye contact with him, then squeezed just enough to make his point.

Nickie didn't offer her hand or a greeting. "I knew," she said to no one in particular, then continued her pacing, this time over the length of the falcon. "Why wait?" The heels of her boots struck the stone in quick, purposeful succession.

Edward rolled his eyes like a teenager, but Nickie hardly noticed. Her focus was directed on the falcon.

"The other girls were taken much younger. Closer to age ten."

"Oh, Nicole." Edward dropped his chin and shook his head. "What have you conjured in your imagination this time?"

"Why wait until I was fourteen?"

Clarence slipped down the same side hallway that Edward and Ivanna had entered. Not without Duncan noticing.

"Does she still do this often, Duncan, my boy? Ramble on incoherently?" Edward shook his hand in front of his face as if a fly were buzzing around his nose. "Done it since she was a little girl, our Nicole."

"I was never your little girl. You made sure of that."

Duncan could see the anger flowing from her body like waves of heat rising from the Middle Eastern desert. She reached into the pocket of her leather jacket, causing both Edward and Ivanna to brace.

She pulled out a sheet of copy paper. Duncan knew what would be on it. Unfolding it, she stepped to her father and held it inches from his face.

Edward craned his neck around it to look at her. "Is this supposed to mean something to me?"

"It's you."

"Yes, I know that, dear. I remember it well. It was at the grand reopening of the IEM building."

"You let him take me," Nickie said. "Or did you arrange it?"

Edward threw up his hands. "Here it comes. Nicole dear, how many times have I recommended therapy to help you recover from what you…did?"

"What I was forced to do as a child to survive?" She shook the paper at them. "You use the term therapist as if it's a bad word," she said and curled her fingers in the air like quotation marks. The printed photo crumpled inside her grasp. "As if there is any human who couldn't use a professional someone to bounce ideas off of? The last one told me she didn't know why I was normal. Best compliment I ever got."

Edward growled, "You were in as much of an agreement as we were when the decision was made for foster home placement."

"Or five foster home placements," Nickie interrupted. "And you haven't answered me."

"We don't know what you're talking about, Nicole," Edward answered. "She does this, Duncan. I hope not too often. We most certainly didn't raise her this way."

"Speaking of raising children properly." Ivanna finally spoke. "Shall we entertain this conversation in the front library like civilized people? Please. We have some lovely chardonnay that could do a world of good."

Duncan started to nod, but Nickie blurted, "No. I am here to get answers. Missing files to my disappearance held by one of your employees. An employee who is the recipient of covert emails about my everyday doings? Mostly, that have to do with this—" She shook the paper of Zheng at him. "—man. An employee of yours who is now six feet under."

"Your people were the last to see Ms. Jacobsen," Edward interrupted. "You were incorrigible then and you continue to act in such a manner. The incorrigible living circumstances weren't healthy for anyone."

"Living circumstances? How deep does this go, Edward? Murder? Abduction? Far enough that Phil the barber had your falcon tattooed on his forearm." She jabbed a finger toward the stones below them.

"Phil the who?" Edward asked. "We don't know what you've concocted this time, but our schedules are very busy."

"Are you going to try and deny that you hid the files regarding my abduction and release? That you arranged for Jun Zheng to take me? At gunpoint? I know about the mole in the department, and who it is. You're going down."

The veins in his Nickie's forehead throbbed under reddened skin. He'd never seen her so shaken or lacking control. She rocked on the balls of her feet as she waited for him to answer.

"We don't know what you're talking about," her mother said. "If you aren't interested in having a civilized conversation, our talk is over."

Nickie snarled, "This shit has only just begun."

The hours-long ride home felt like minutes. The three flights of stairs to their master bedroom like miles. Nickie didn't want to talk and was thankful she didn't have to explain that to Duncan. Enough had been said at her parents' home. Nickie knew what had to happen next. A search of the place…legal or not.

She paused at Xena's empty crate. It was too late to pick her up from Duncan's brother even if he did live just down the lane.

Her father worked for Jun Zheng. It was advertised in stone over his entire foyer. She let herself fall onto the ottoman at the end of her bed. She'd lost her temper.

Duncan kept an eye on her as he changed out of his clothes. He was the best thing this world had given her. Ignoring the buttons on her shirt, her heavy arms pulled it over her head. People get sloppy when they lose their tempers. It could never happen again.

Nothing was coincidence. Her childhood abduction with no signs of forced entry. The files that said so that went missing. Her father's employee who was found with the missing files. The employee who lay in her grave from a gunshot to her temple. And the photo of her father and her abductor. Her captor. Nickie clenched the edge of the ottoman.

The water was running in the bathroom. She hadn't noticed that he'd gone in there. She let out a sigh of defeat and took off the rest of her clothes. After all of it, her father continued to point fingers at her so-called imagination and fabrications. Leaving the pile of clothes where they lay, she pulled back the sheets and slipped into bed.

He thought he was above the law. Edward had gotten away with this for so many years, he didn't think he could be touched by a small town female detective. Certainly not by a trafficking victim. And absolutely not by his daughter. He was going to pay for it all. She closed her eyes. Let the nightmares be damned. He would pay for all of the girls. The pain of all of the children.

Duncan turned out the lights and crawled in next to her. He turned her away from him, then curled in behind. His damp, lanky body pressed into her.

"You're like a battery," she said.

His cheek spread against her shoulder.

"You're smiling. I am serious."

He responded by wrapping his arms around her and pulling her into him tighter.

Weight left her arms and legs and heart. "Dave is going to be pissed as hell that we didn't take him with."

"You didn't take him with."

Now she was smiling. "Okay, chicken. I didn't take him with. It crossed state lines. Which was the problem with taking him. There was nothing he could do legally, and much that could get him in deep water." Although it was pitch black, she twisted in his arms to face him.

"But, I told him I would bring him, and now we need to return and with backup."

"I assumed this is where your plans were taking you."

"There are FBI Special Agents Goodrich and Hurst. The trip would be right up their alley. I wouldn't even need to call in favors to get the warrant with them involved."

"Special Agent Hurst might take it personally that you didn't involve him today."

She frowned in the dark. "No. It was my childhood home. I had sound, plausible reason to show my husband around the place. Or, in this case, search the place. Captain Dave? Not so much. It was a wasted trip," she said and collapsed on her pillow. "We didn't even get a chance to look around."

"I don't believe it was wasted."

The blanket of calm that was her husband covered her more than the sheets. Her eyes adjusted to the dark, and she focused on the outline of his face, using the peace, the energy and clarity that came with it. "We don't know any more now than we did this morning," she said as sleep tried to take her. "The fact that they allowed me to be taken at the late age of fourteen is significant, and we don't know the whys behind it," she slurred. "I'm missing something, Duncan."

"I know an excellent hypnotist."

Her eyes opened wide. "Did you just say, 'Hypnotist'?"

"Do you have an aversion to hypnotism?" he asked and kissed her forehead.

"Do I?" she answered, then shrugged against the sheets. Maybe it was worth a try. What could it hurt? Other than the idea that lifelong suppressed childhood secrets might come out mid-session. "Maybe," she whispered and rolled away from him again. He would know that maybe meant yes. And if she wasn't half asleep, she might have called him out on it.

He laid his lips on the side of her neck, causing her semi-conscious state to seep into a puddle. Lanky fingers traced circles down her arm. She may have crooned in response, but she wasn't sure. His warm lips drew lazy lines down her neck and over her bare shoulder.

She should reciprocate. It was the right thing to do. She would. Soon. Just as soon as the electricity finished its cycle through her body and her arms and legs obeyed her commands. Instead, she snuggled into him, discovering that he wanted her as much as she wanted this. Wanted him.

As she reached behind, a single quick breath brushed the back of her hair. His fingers paused for a short moment before they continued to explore. A thumb grazed the side of her breast before his entire hand encompassed her.

Her eyes crossed. Her toes curled. He was like a drug. She had to have more. Fingers circled her before gently pulling, making her back arch into him. His hand snaked down her stomach, leaving a trail of heat over her hip before taking hold of the place between her thigh and backside.

It was as if her legs had minds of their own, squirming to lead him to the place that called to him. He cupped his hand over her and, "Oh." The peak was instant, long and lazy. Her mind sank into nirvana, blissfully void of anything that had taken her to dark places that day.

She came down like slow-moving lava, his fingers in tandem with her diminishing aftershocks. His lips brushed the side of her neck, his warm breath quickening. He started to bring her back up that climb, but in her groggy resolve, she tucked back into him, using his need for her in order to change his course of action. He caved and slipped into her. One hand grasped her shoulder, the other her hip. It was slow and deep and with more love than she knew her heart could hold.

They rose together as one, as lovers. As mister and missus. Rose until she wanted to fly away with him and live like this forever. She crossed an arm over her chest, reaching for his hand. Clasping her fingers in his, she found the closeness that came only with love.

She pulled him to her and heard him suck in air. He dug his forehead into her shoulder, pressing into the last inch closer. Her body shook and held. The grasp she had on his fingers slowly releasing as her mind began to drift. She felt his lips press against her shoulder and his arms wrap around her. For tonight, she was safe. She was loved.

CHAPTER 10

Nickie stopped just inside the entrance to the Santiago Center for Mental Health. She leaned forward, checking around the place. The lights were on in the reception area, but not a single person was anywhere to be found. Some doc place this turned out to be.

Duncan placed an open hand on her back and gestured with his chin toward the door on the far side of the room. The only reason she didn't run from the room was because this was the doc Duncan used for his PTSD.

She shrugged and moved with purpose deeper into the room. The doctor's office door was open. The light was on. She knocked anyway.

A female voice called out from the room, "Come in."

Nickie took a few steps into the place, then sank her hands into her pockets and rocked back on her heels. The room was pleasant, of course. A few floor plants. Neutral colors.

The gal came over and held out a hand.

Confused, Nickie pulled her chin back, but offered her hand in return. "I'm Detective Nickie Savage. I'm here to see Dr. Santiago."

"This is her," Duncan said. "Dr. Santiago, this is Nickie Savage. Nickie, this is Dr. Santiago."

"He's a she?" Nickie asked. "Oh," she corrected. "Sorry and all that. Duncan spoke of you before. I just assumed you were a…ya know…a guy."

The doc was a she. Nickie looked up and to the right, trying to readjust her months-long perception of Duncan's doctor. Had Nickie become a chauvinist?

The doc was as feminine as feminine could be. Loose linen slacks with a matching blouse and long pearl necklace that drooped over the buttons of the shirt. Her hair hung loose in long wavy auburn curls.

"Nope," the doctor said. "I'm all girl. And please call me Lara. Shall we?" Lara? Duncan always called her Dr. Santiago.

Stepping aside, Lara gestured to the interior of the room.

Nickie looked around. "No dim lights? No candles? Where do you want me?"

Duncan placed his hand around her upper arm. She looked up at him. His scowl was back.

Nickie needed some air. She needed to go outside and start over.

"Wherever you'd like, really," Lara said as she walked to a wet bar and opened the door to a mini-fridge.

Nickie assessed the options. She skipped the couch and chose a straight-back chair on the other side of a low bamboo coffee table.

"Would you care for something to drink?" Lara asked. "Coffee? Tea? Duncan mentioned you prefer Diet Coke."

"Water'd be great. Thanks." Nickie partially lowered in the chair, held herself up using the armrests, crossed her boots under her backside, then sat on her feet.

Duncan avoided the couch, too, and chose the seat across the table.

The doc took three bottles from the mini-fridge and said, "Can you tell me why you think you have repressed memories?"

Pulling her chin back again, Nickie lowered her brows. "I don't think I have repressed memories." Duncan was the one who thought so. "I think there are some details from when I was a kid that I don't remember."

"Nickie," Duncan started, but the doctor interrupted him.

"No, it's fine. That makes sense. Tell me why you think hypnosis might aid in clarifying some details from when you were a kid."

Nickie shrugged. "I guess you could say I'm stuck. Figure it can't hurt."

"Thank you for your honesty." She handed one of the bottles to Nickie and the other to Duncan. Sitting in the middle of the couch, she twisted open her bottle and took a sip.

Hey. Nickie was the patient. The couch was supposed to be her spot.

"Exactly what kinds of questions would you like me to ask? What answers are you hoping to learn?"

Nickie looked at Duncan. He dipped his head once and blinked a long blink. "I think there was something that happened when I was fourteen that made my father decide to get rid of me."

Impressively, the doc didn't look away, wince or even blink an eye at the unusual accusation. Had Duncan told her all this already? Of course he had. She wouldn't be able to tell that to Nickie. Doctor/patient confidentiality and all that. The doctor leaned back and crossed her legs at the knees. "Did he ever do anything inappropriate with you other than try to get rid of you?"

Nickie sighed and shook her head. What a question. "He doesn't show any of the signs of being a pedophile, if that's what you mean." She stopped and looked Lara in the eye. "I know the signs. I am guessing Duncan told you a lot about me. This would work better if you told me what you know."

Lara paused. Nickie guessed her question wasn't protocol. "That is completely fair." She tilted her head to the side; just barely, but it was there. She smiled slightly and said, "I know you were abducted at gun point from your home at the age of fourteen. For eighteen months, you were held captive and forced into prostitution." Lara nodded before she continued. "You are responsible for the rescue of twenty-five trafficked children in and out of the state. You've aided in the rehabilitation of these children as well as the preventative education for local high school and college students. I would say I trust that you know the signs well."

All details she could have gotten from public records, but Nickie understood the drill. She released her boots from their prison beneath her body and set them on the floor. "The education part is from Child Rescue. Not me."

"The national trafficking education, rescue and rehabilitation organization."

Nodding, Nickie continued. "Yes. A local college rape victim wanted to make a difference and went through training with them. She gives regular workshops for high school and college kids regarding strategies to keep safe."

Duncan smiled warmly.

"The girl, the rape victim, has trained three young women to be trainers and is creating a web of available educational sessions and resources. She's completely amazing."

"As is someone who chooses a life of detective work in order to save as many victims of abuse and abduction as possible."

"Fair enough," Nickie said, using Lara's words back at her. "So, is it okay if we get started?"

Duncan noticed as his Nickie pressed her knuckles against her chin and pushed until there was a crack. It was what she did when she was a mixture of uneasy and angry or frustrated. Duncan assumed there was a combination of all three.

"I'm sure you can tell this is uncomfortable for me," Nickie said. "I apologize for my abruptness."

"Apology accepted." Dr. Santiago's smile was sincere. "I'm fascinated with your change in speech register and posture since the time you walked in. I assume your parents were well-to-do? Is the abruptness a defense against that upbringing?" Dr. Santiago dipped her chin and shook her head. "That's not me getting started. My turn to apologize. You're a fascinating woman, Detective Savage. I'd love to hear all about your story some time."

"Call me Nickie, and apology accepted."

"You want to know the details of the night you were abducted," Dr. Santiago said.

Nickie shook her head. "Nah. I have enough of that." She tapped the side of her head. "I just can't remember parts of the before." A smile spread across her face. "I may have repressed an event or two within the confines of my childhood home that caused my father to either allow or arrange for my abduction. As you mentioned, I was fourteen. This is significantly older than the age of the girls this particular crime ring normally takes as captives."

It was as if Duncan wasn't there. This was a good thing. Nickie was beginning to relax, possibly even beginning to like Dr. Santiago.

"And you are certain your parents either allowed or arranged for your abduction?"

Nickie nodded. "No signs of forced entry. My father hid the files of my abduction and escape. Hired a mole within the station. We have a photo of him with my abductor. Years after my escape." She let her lungs fill with air. "Will saying this shit ever get easier?"

"Yes. It's part of what keeps me employed. You don't have enough evidence to arrest your father?" Dr. Santiago threw her hand up like she was forfeiting a game. "Can I take that back? Not only have I learned about your childhood, but I have also learned about your impressive record of solid casework."

"I have to tell ya. I'm not so sure this will work. My mind isn't like regular minds."

"Understandable. We'll see what we can do. Do you trust me?"

"I'll be honest with you. I trust him," Nickie said, pointing to Duncan.

It was a trust he would never betray. I love you, he mouthed. She didn't scoff at the display of affection.

"Can you give me a physical description of the house?"

"Wow. Okay. Big, really big. Stone. Clammy. Cold. Grays. Blacks and some browns."

Dr. Santiago lifted her brows. "Wow back at you. That was perfect. Are you comfortable with the description of the room you were taken from?"

"If you say so. It was also big, although the bed was a twin. Bunk bed. I slept on the bottom. No one slept on the top."

"Ever?"

"Ever. Window at the foot of the bed and to the left. The bed had posts at the corners with white sashes dropping from each." With each word, Nickie's eyes closed in thought. "The comforter was white with white ringlets covering it. Three more windows were spaced after the one at the foot of the bed…the one I was taken from. A walk-in closet was at the end of the room opposite my bed. And on the other side of the wall with the windows were two tall dressers with a long mirror and powder table between them."

"Thank you, Nickie. Were the colors also blacks and grays in this room?"

"Yes. The outside wall was stone. The rest painted drywall. I covered the stones between the windows with posters of rock stars."

"Tell me about the days before you were taken."

Nickie shrugged and opened her eyes. "That's what I'm here for. I got nothin'."

Dr. Santiago nodded. "How about a general day, then?"

"Right. Um. Me sneaking around the house. It was summer. No school. I had cello lessons and riding lessons. Horses. English style. I used to sneak to the barn and ride bareback every chance I got. It made my parents insane."

They went on like this longer than Duncan would have imagined. He learned much that was new about his wife and could have listened for twice the time.

"I want you to close your eyes now, Nickie. I'm going to say some words and ask you to concentrate fully on them.

Please try to create a picture in your mind of what I describe. Are you ready?"

"Here? I just sit here?"

Dr. Santiago smiled. "Would you be more comfortable laying down? I assumed you chose the chair for a reason."

"Nope. I'm good." She circled her shoulders a few times. "Give it your best shot."

"It's simple, really. Just close your eyes. Concentrate on your breathing. I'm going to describe a landscape for you. See if you can create a picture of it in your mind."

CHAPTER 11

Duncan sat studying Nickie's posture, the muscles in her face, her body. It broke his heart into icy, jagged pieces. He watched helplessly as she struggled between protecting deep secrets and her need to learn how much her father was involved in her abduction and Fu Haizi.

Her head and shoulders remained stiff, yet still. Her eyes darted behind closed lids. Dr. Santiago spoke of noisy brooks in tepid weather. Her voice lit a metaphorical stick of incense beneath him that nearly caused Duncan to go under himself.

"I'm going to ask you to remember when you were a little girl," she said in a low voice. "Do you remember being a little girl, Nickie?"

"Yes," she answered. Duncan wasn't sure if she was under or not until she said, "My name is Nicole." Present tense. He didn't care if it made sense for her to say it; he couldn't stand it.

"That's good, Nicole. I want you to think about the time you turned fourteen. You had a horse and a cello. Do you remember?"

"Yes. The horses." Nickie smiled, but it quickly turned into a frown. "My mother, like, doesn't let me have time with them unless I, like, play my cello in the school orchestra. She tries to get me a new cello every year, but I use my old one."

"That's good, Nicole. Very good. Something happened around that time. Something you think made your father let Jun Zheng take you." The doctor had mirrored Nickie's mindset and changed to present tense.

Nickie's shoulders pulled forward and her voice changed to that of a much younger Nickie. "He's a very bad man."

Duncan ground his teeth together. He might not make it through this.

"Yes, he is."

"He calls me a savage."

"I remember that," Dr. Santiago lied. "But I want you to think of before you met Jun Zheng. Before you were taken. Can you think of why they want him to take you?"

"They are mad at me." She nodded. "They don't like me."

"That must be hard for you."

"It hurts me, but I tell myself it doesn't."

"I see. It hurts your heart. That's a bad kind of hurt, Nicole, and I'm sorry to hear it. Did they ever hurt the outside of your body?"

She shook her head. "No. They don't care enough about me to spank me or anything. If I could just walk better and dress better, they might like me. I sneak into the barn and ride the horses after dark. They only want me to ride English style, but I don't," she said in her early teen Nickie voice.

"Why do you think they let Jun Zheng take you from your bedroom? You were older than most of the girls he takes."

"I found the puppy room," Nickie said as if the question was obvious.

Duncan's brows lowered and he sighed, but the doctor seemed quite the opposite of discouraged.

"Tell me about the day you found the puppy room. What is it like?"

"There are computers and places for puppies to sleep."

"That's good, Nicole. Tell me more."

"The computers are on one side of the room. They are big. One, two, three, four. There are four. They all match and are yellowish whitish. The room has rocks for walls, and the floor is gray and hard."

"That's good. Thank you."

"I can't get caught. I'm not supposed to be down here. I do naughty stuff like this. It's why they don't like me. I think the man sees me in here. I bet he's going to tell on me now. He's like that. They won't let me ride the horses for a month when they find out I'm in here." Nickie pulled up her knees and wrapped her arms around them. "Oh no, he's coming."

"Who is coming, Nicole?"

Her eyes flew open, and she slapped her right hand over her mouth. Focusing on a spot on the far wall, she whimpered, "They put me in the red room this time." Releasing the grip on her legs with her other hand, she shook it out, then clasped and opened her fingers again and again.

The dream. Oh, please no. She'd moved to the dream. Waving his hand at the doctor, he gained her attention. "This is a recurring nightmare she has."

"They put me in a bright yellow bra with matching panties. That was what they liked to call them. I don't even have any boobs for a bra. They want me to look like I am a virgin. They took that from me a long time ago."

Nickie didn't notice as Duncan waved a frantic signal for the doctor to stop.

"This one likes me. They brought him to me before. He calls me Savage like the rest of them. I'll show him a savage." Tears ran freely down her cheeks.

Duncan clenched the sides of his chair to keep from jumping to his wife and taking her in his arms.

The doctor sat still. "Nicole, I'm going to wake you now."

Nickie changed her voice to imitate that of a male, an adult male. "That's a good one, Mr. Kruger."

A name. Duncan stood and held up a single hand, palm out. "No, wait," he said to the doctor. Conflict tore at his heart, his mind, his gut. "What is the man's first name, Nickie—?" He shook his head and corrected himself. "Nicole. What's the man's first name, Nicole?"

Nickie ignored him.

Dr. Santiago spoke as if this was normal, as if this could possibly somehow have been frigging normal. "Nicole, can you tell me Mr. Kruger's whole name? What is his first name, honey?"

"George. He's coming. I have to be ready. I have to be like a savage. Tonight, I'm going to kill him."

"Wake her up," Duncan said, bolting to his feet. "Wake her up now."

Tears of surrender flowed down Nickie's perfect face. Pulling her legs tight, she wrapped both arms around them, clamped her eyes shut again and curled in a fetal position. "I hate this. I hate this. I hate this," she said as she buried her head in her knees and rocked.

"Do you want me to have her remember when she wakes, Duncan?"

He couldn't get any words to come from his throat. Heat pulsed through him. She'd told him she wanted to remember. Waves of hot guilt and confusion weighed him back to a sitting position. He put his face in his hands and nodded.

"He's so fat, I can't tell if he has a belt on. I need him to have a belt on so I can kill him with it."

Duncan's eyes burned. He shook as his mouth craned downward.

"Not tonight, Nicole. I'm going to get you out of that room now. You can leave that place and come back to my office. I'm letting you. You're going to wake up when I finish counting to three. You're going to remember everything you told me, but you are going to leave that room and wake up. Are you ready?"

Duncan couldn't bear to see if she nodded.

"One, two, three."

* * *

R.T. Wolfe

"I'm sorry," Nickie said and waved her hand like she was shooing a fly. "This was never going to work. I don't know how to take down this cocoon I seem to crawl into. That's what Gloria calls it—"

Her arms. Why were they sweaty? And her scalp and back. Her feet were on the chair. Her knees up high. She set one boot on the floor, then the other. "George Kruger," she said. "Who is George Kruger, and why am I thinking of that name?"

She glanced at Duncan. His expression. It scared her. What had she said? No, what had she done?

Air sucked into her lungs. It was like trying to breathe ice-cold water. "George Kruger." Her eyes went to Lara. "You asked me about the dream! About that night? That was not part of the agreement!" She tried to stand, but her legs gave out on her, and she fell back to her chair.

"She didn't," Duncan interrupted, his voice cracking. "You went there. I told her to let you." He looked away from her to the other side of the room. "I told her to let you remember."

"Alcohol. Cigarettes and sweat. I can smell him." Childhood tears ran down her cheeks that were already wet and raw. "George Kruger."

She looked at the back of Duncan's head as his shoulders trembled. She stood on shaky legs and made her way to him like he was a perp who might bolt. Part of her wanted to bury her head in his shoulder and part of her wanted to beat him with her fists.

"I should have told the doctor to keep those memories in your subconscious where they belong."

"No," she said, settling for taking his hand and grasping it as hard as she could. "I told you to make me remember."

He responded by turning to her and wrapping his free hand around her shoulders, pulling her into him. She dug her face into his neck, inhaling deeply as she tried to erase the scent of George Kruger, whom she murdered. They stayed like this long enough that she forgot Lara was there.

"Can you tell us about the puppies?" the doctor asked.

Her chest released the breath she didn't know she'd been holding. She maneuvered between Duncan's knees and sat on the floor in front of him. Lara waited for Nickie to calm her breathing. "There were no puppies," she answered.

Closing her eyes, she craned her head away from Lara. "It's what I saw as a child. What I perceived. The room was a holding facility." She paused to keep herself from hyperventilating. "The cages held children who were being conditioned to do what they were told. There were mattresses used for the same purpose. Different tactic."

"And the computers?"

"I don't know." She needed a shower. And food. She was so hungry. She needed a shower and some food and sleep. "They must have used the room for some kind of bookwork." It was all making sense now. "And it must have been why my parents needed to get rid of me. I was a witness. The rich runaway story kept attention away from what was going on in the place."

But the falcon in the foyer. The matching tattoo on Phil the barber's forearm? She never remembered anything like it on Jun Zheng's body, not that she'd ever seen him undressed. He didn't use her for that. Only beatings. Her empty stomach couldn't take much more.

"I'm going to that room," she said. "Very soon."

Nickie shuffled through soggy leaves. Xena had done such a good job last week of coming back after chasing the small herd of deer, Nickie decided to try her without a leash. Good dog. Xena was too young to be this good. She must be gifted.

Dampness seeped through Nickie's shoes and soaked her feet. She should have worn the waterproof boots Duncan bought her, but they were winter boots and it was entering the dead of summer in upstate New York. She'd rather have wet socks.

She promised her captain she would keep him appraised of her every move. And the ADA. And Duncan and Gloria and Andy and Rose. The crawling into a cocoon thing never worked anymore. Not with her family and friends or with keeping her from being hypnotized.

The john she killed gave her the creeps more than her father's involvement. Hearing his voice, his name. She would never forget the stench she remembered when she was hypnotized. Was this what Duncan dealt with on a daily basis? Of course it was. It had drained her of all physical, emotional and spiritual energy.

Xena lifted her snout at a cracking twig. "Come on, girl," Nickie said before curiosity trumped obedience. As if to give a warning, Xena let out a quick woof at the offending branch before trotting on next to her.

George Kruger. She shivered and not from the wet socks. What happened to his body? What was the story created to explain his death? Was it reported as a murder? Why hadn't she found anything resembling it? With a name, she would find the john. He might be in the form of a missing person's case, but she would find him.

Tonight, she would spend at home.

Home.

CHAPTER 12

Xena sniffed every tree and spot she passed, but didn't move from Nickie's left side. "Good girl," Nickie said and scratched beneath Xena's ears. Nickie turned, walked faster, then slowed to a stroll all while the girl remained at her left side.

Nickie was officially one of those moms who was unreasonably proud of her girl.

Mom.

Duncan's desire for children had clotheslined her. He left her birth control pills in the center of the kitchen table. It was the spot they placed objects that needed discussion. He had much too much faith in her potential parenting abilities. Just because she could train a Rottweiler didn't mean she could be a good mom to a kid.

She hadn't taken the pills in weeks. It left a consistent, uneasy tension in the back of her shoulders. And when was the last time she had a swig of crisp, cold carbonation? The caffeine withdrawal headache had been something she wouldn't have wished on her worst enemy.

More importantly, why hadn't she told Duncan any of it? She sighed and stepped around a cluster of saplings that inhibited her sight of their deck. Maybe her cocoon remained intact. Could be a good thing, or maybe not.

As if she knew Nickie had been thinking about her, Xena lifted her head and sniffed about a dozen times in quick succession. "It's the grill, little one." Hundred-twenty-pound little one. "It's just Dad. He's making us dinner."

Dad.

Duncan was a shoo-in for the position. Raised in a family who loved him. Siblings, a dog, even a creek in the backyard to play in.

He stood over their grill, poking at the charcoals with a stick. He was the sexiest, smartest, most intuitive person she'd ever known. And he loved her.

"Go on, girl," she said to Xena. The pup gave her a look as if she hated it when humans spoke English words she didn't know. "Release," Nickie amended.

Xena took off through the last fifty yards of brush to the deck. The wet pads of her feet slipped on the stairs. She stumbled, fell and regained her footing all without stopping the momentum of her full-grown body.

Duncan squatted, grabbed hold of her cheeks and rubbed. Nickie couldn't hear what he was saying, but Xena sank her backside to the deck floor and rubbed faces with him before taking off inside.

As Nickie climbed the stairs, the distinct sound of a sloppy tongue lapping water came from the kitchen. "I almost came looking for you," Duncan said as he balanced a plate of steaks in one hand and stabbed them with the spear in his other before placing them on the grill.

"I decided to check around for more clues to the case of the black glove." She raised her brows up and down. "Slippery Jimbo calls me Sherman Holmes."

"Ouch. Let us discuss anyone other than James this evening." He winked at her. "Any luck with the black glove?"

"Nope. All the clues are washed away from the rain we've had."

She stopped and admired his backside as he shifted his weight while fooling with the grill. When he finally noticed her staring at him, he did a double take. The rare smile that erupted across his face made her breath catch.

"You're beautiful," he said, stepping toward her. His arms were a safety net, taking her away from all that was deceptive and wrong.

"And you are light." She dug her cheek into his collarbone, inhaling the scent of him deep into her lungs. "A circle of peace surrounds you everywhere you go. I find myself trying to step into it more each day."

"Mmm," he crooned in his low voice. The side of his thumb pressed into the back of her neck, drawing a line from the base of her skull to her tailbone. Certain parts of her body woke, making her all but forget dinner and the dog.

Slithering her arms up his back, she took in the strength that radiated through the muscle. "I haven't had a Diet Coke in three weeks," she confessed before realizing the magnitude of the statement.

He pulled away and took her shoulders in his hands. It made her laugh. He squinted his eyes as if she'd told him she had a life threatening illness.

His voice was low. "What are you laughing at?"

"Your reaction."

"Are you going to become a vegan as well?" he asked, fishing for more information.

"That's not why I'm suffering without aspartame and caffeine. I haven't taken a pill since you put them on the kitchen table."

His fingers gripped her shoulders tighter. He pushed her away to arm's length, then thrust her against his chest. "You mean…?" he whispered in her ear as his long arms encompassed her.

"Can't…breathe…Duncan." Sheesh, it was true.

He released her and took her face in his warm hands. "Are you sure about this?"

"Of course I'm not sure." She smiled. "I have no idea what to do, say, feel. Definitely not what to do."

He sucked in a deep breath and pressed his hips to her. He'd gone rock hard in three seconds. His gaze dropped to her lips. "I can help with that."

"That's not the do I'm talking about. I mean the parenting kind of do."

He moved one of his hands to run a thumb over her bottom lip. "You're a natural with Xena."

She squinted a single eye closed. "You did not just compare parenting children to raising a dog."

"What about Nevaeh?"

"Okay. So, if I don't ruin them by the time they reach college, I might be an all right mother."

"You said mother." He pressed his forehead against hers, then rotated his head from one side to the other. He wrapped his arms around her once again. It was possessive. The good kind of possessive. He pulled his head back and looked into her eyes like he'd had an epiphany. "And what about Lela and baby Jorge?"

"Jorge is the twin Teresa gave me to hold? I can never tell the difference between two. I said okay to this family thing, but I'm counting on you to keep me grounded and take up the slack every time I mess up." She was suddenly quite interested in the baby-making process. "Maybe we should get started on the trying while the steaks cook?"

She let her hand travel down his chest and abs, then took hold of said rock-hard parts. The air left his lungs, and his hips responded, pressing deeper against her.

His hands. His glorious hands. They kneaded and explored, traveling into her hair, over her shoulders and around her backside. She couldn't let go. The feel of him in her hands was an aphrodisiac. Or was it the idea of doing this with a purpose beyond pleasure? Instinct took over logic.

Their lips twined, gaining momentum in sync with their breathing. It was like the first time. A quick, raw need. The weaving of limbs and mouths. His warm, needy lips left hers and trailed a line of wet across her jaw to beneath her ear.

She opened her eyes to the top of his head of dark brown hair as his desperate lips invaded the neck of her blouse. Bright orange coals caught her eyes. "Wait a minute," she panted with disappointment dripping from her voice. "There are four steaks."

"Anybody home?" a voice called as it came from around the side of the house.

Duncan shrugged his shoulders. "My brother called when you were walking Xena."

As if to yell, "No," she let her head fall back. Xena barked loud enough to make them both jump before tearing down the stairs of the deck. A few feet before reaching Andy and his wife, she leapt. Andy was nimble. He carried a large poster board thing in his hand yet still skirted out of the way and in front of Rose just in time. Xena would have surely knocked both of them to the ground.

"So much for gifted," Nickie mumbled.

"Xena, sit," Rose said in her voice that said she worked with animals for a living. Regardless of the fact that she didn't reach five foot tall and was also carrying a baby, Xena sat and dropped her snout. "You're a good girl, aren't you?" Rose scratched Xena's cheek as she spoke. "You just get excited to see Uncle Andy and Aunt Rose."

Opening her fingers, Rose placed her hand several inches from Xena's nose and said, "Stay." Giving Andy a small shove, she walked to the base of the deck stairs. Andy climbed to the top, but Rose waited, holding baby A.J.

"Please stay, please stay, please stay," Nickie chanted quietly.

Rose said, "Xena, come." The dog took off and closed the few yards between them.

Breathing a sigh of relief, Nickie said, "Come on in. It's been too long."

"That's what we said." Andy slid the poster board along the wall just inside the French doors leading into the house. He strolled over to the grill and sniffed. "Smells good, brother."

Duncan nodded his gratitude but still hadn't spoken a word. His eyes were on the house.

"So, what's this about connecting Edward Monticello to Jun Zheng?" Andy asked.

Nickie sighed. Her sex buzz was so over.

"I finished tracking paths left from the emails Eddy Lynx sent and received from the laptop and tower you illegally sneaked out of the station." Andy spoke a mile a minute, as he liked to do. "Just the ones that led to the source at Edward Monticello's business." Andy squinted his eyes. "How did you get away with taking the machines anyway?"

He was careful not to refer to Edward as her father. She hated when people did that. "If I told you, I'd have to kill you."

The smell from the grill made her stomach growl. She wanted to think about food or her guests or the fact that Xena wasn't at all acting like a gifted dog. But Duncan had rotated on the balls of his feet and took three long strides to get to the French doors that led into their kitchen. Even though she tried to catch up with him, it took her twice as many steps.

"I told Andy you wouldn't be able to wait until after dinner," Rose said to Duncan as she bounced A.J. on her hip and pulled plates from the cabinet.

Duncan slid the poster from its hiding spot and studied it as he strolled to their enormous kitchen table. His head turned from one side to the other, the way he did when he created theories or made connections.

"Duncan?"

He stood with arms crossed and legs locked.

She stepped next to him. Sheesh. How much time did this take Andy? It was unbelievable. The poster was a map of North and South America. Covering it was a complicated maze of hundreds of lines that zigzagged from city to city, state to state and country to country.

"The loser didn't use international locations other than North and South America," Andy said as he stepped next to his brother. "What do you think, Duncan?"

"Look at the clusters," Duncan said, pointing to areas where several dozen lines converged, crisscrossing each other in clusters.

Detroit, St. Louis, Seattle, Austin, Tampa and…she craned her head closer…Henderson, Nevada. Duncan dipped his nose near the same spot. Together, they turned their chins until their eyes met.

"Henderson," they said at the same time.

CHAPTER 13

Nickie wanted to sling a boot across her knee and crack her neck, but this was Captain Nolan she was talking to. He was more than her captain; he was her friend, her mentor. For him, she would be helpful and sit professionally with her ankles crossed and hands folded.

"Right," her captain said in a tone that wasn't at all professional or helpful. "You don't like to share."

Rain fell in sheets against the floor-to-ceiling windows that lined the back of Dave's office. The clouds leaking the buckets were dark enough to make it seem like night. So much for helpful. She couldn't take it anymore and let her head fall back. "I didn't say I wouldn't do it," she whined to the ceiling.

"I know you'll do it. It's a direct order."

She hated when he pulled rank.

"I need you to agree to full disclosure."

Dr. Traci Li. Profiler borrowed from the city now and then. A female, no less. This warranted another childish sigh. "I agree, I agree." Mostly. Almost completely.

"Good, because she's in Interrogation 1."

Now? Opening her eyes, she let her chin drop enough to see if he was serious. Damn it. There it was. True concern, love and trust. It was why she'd been avoiding eye contact since he paged her to his office…professionally, of course.

"She's meeting with the ADA about a case Miranda's working on."

"But we know who we're trying to arrest. Jun Zheng, Edward Monticello and Eddy Lynx. In that order."

"I want you to get to the bottom of the trafficking, Nick. You know how much I do."

Yes, but did he realize it was her purpose in all of this? In life?

"First, I need to find Lynx. Where the hell is he? We haven't heard a damned thing. Dr. Li might give us insight we've overlooked. It would be careless not to use her while we've got her here."

Did he have to make sense all of the time? "Interrogation?" she whined.

It was odd to watch a man of his status who was well over six foot and two hundred pounds roll his eyes. "I couldn't have her performing her interviews and going through files in the break room, now could I?"

Nickie's files would be incomplete. Dave knew this. Which was why he wanted her to speak with Dr. Li. To spill her deep, dark family secrets.

Plopping her boots flat on the floor, she slapped her hands on her thighs and stood. "I won't let you down." She meant it.

The walk to interrogation was too short to gather her composure and too long to sweep the imagery under the carpet. She pulled her cell from her pocket and scrolled through her contacts. She stopped at the S's. Slippery Jimbo. Hating that she even had him in her contacts, she dialed.

He answered after the first damned ring. It was morning, and he answered on the first ring. Granted, it was almost noon, but this was Slippery Jimbo. Slicked back hair, T & A bar t-shirt, trench coat-wearing thief, Slippery Jimbo. "Official Police Informant Jimbo speaking." And he read his Caller ID.

"Any word on Eddy Lynx?"

"No good morning, Detective Dude? Just right to business? Okay. Nope. Nada. And I've got eyes, Detective Dude. Nothing from Phil the barber's old place either."

"Call me if you see or hear anything."

"Will do, Detecti—"

She hung up at the sight of Officer Parker towering just outside of Interrogation 1. He looked like he was guarding Buckingham Palace.

Nickie lifted her brows to him. "Miranda's in there now?"

He blushed and nodded twice. Damnedest thing she'd ever seen.

"Ya know, it's not weird anymore." Much.

"Pardon me, sir?" He blinked and jerked his head toward her. "Ma'am? I mean, Detective?"

"You and the ADA."

Shaking his head, Parker said, "I…um."

Confident, coordinated Officer Dale Parker tripping over his words. It was worth every minute. "And no, no one knows about your little tryst in the closet. Your secret is safe with me." And something she would never be able to unsee. And here she thought he couldn't get any redder.

The door opened. The ADA came out. No one followed her. First she glanced at Parker. Then, at Nickie. "What did you say to him?" she asked.

"Who, me?" Nickie said with a grin.

Miranda's lungs expanded, then released. "The captain told me to have Dr. Li stay in there when we were done. I assumed it was for your case. Or cases. Would you like me to sit in with you?"

"Nah. I've got this. Thanks." Truth be told, Nickie didn't trust her. Yet. She looked up to Parker. "You too, man. Thanks for everything."

With both of them red in the face now, they turned and headed for the elevators, walking two feet apart.

Nickie stepped in front of the metal door to Interrogation 1. She stopped, took a deep breath and turned the knob.

* * *

"You didn't have to come," Duncan said, although he always enjoyed his brother's company.

"You said you needed to talk, brother. I haven't been to one of these things in years."

On the drive to Rochester, conversation had rested mostly on their aunt and uncle, the cousins who were siblings to them and Andy's son, A.J. Duncan's desire for family ties seemed to increase exponentially with age.

"Today is simply a pre-show endorsement." Ever since Duncan's first showing at the Whitham Museum of Art, the board assumed he would be back on a yearly basis.

"I'm not at all certain why my manager insists I approve of the display beforehand. This is what I pay him to do. Regardless, I am grateful you came with me, because yes, I'd like to discuss some ideas."

Rain came down in buckets, making the trip north slower than Duncan's Jaguar F 550 LIP was comfortable traveling. They turned the corner onto the final road leading to the venue. Traditional wrought iron streetlamps burned yellow through the darkened sky.

A bolt of lightning lit the front of the expansive building. It resembled the Lincoln Memorial. Rectangular, three stories tall, with rows of windows and soldiered pillars, each reaching the top of the structure.

"Whoa," Andy said. "Marble and white pillars. It's nice to get away from mud and excavation equipment for a while."

Andy's building development and design company. Duncan took him away from it. "You've always been there for me. Even when I wasn't."

Duncan turned into the museum's patron lot. It didn't open until noon. Yet out of respect, he maneuvered his Jag into a customer spot. "I asked you to take a day for me. Again. And, technically, it isn't for me. Again."

"Oh no, you don't. Nickie is like blood to me. What she's been through…that's messed up. She doesn't let it break her."

"It's why she does what she does. And why she is who she is."

"Some people get bitter. Some get better."

Andy understood. He always understood.

Andy shrugged. "What do you think about the map?"

The maze of lines crisscrossing over North and South America.

"I could tell your mind was going places the night I brought it over," Andy continued as he took off his seat belt and zipped his brown leather jacket. "You have an idea about it. I could tell."

Duncan nodded. "Let's talk as we walk." He cracked his door and stuck his umbrella through the space. Releasing the latch, he stepped out beneath it as rain thrummed the material and the fresh, damp air filled his lungs.

Andy waved off the offer to share the umbrella, and they jogged through the rain, avoiding puddles on the way to the wide, marble staircase leading to the main entrance.

The door was unlocked. Duncan shook his umbrella before setting it near the coatroom inside the entrance. An employee Duncan didn't recognize came out of the office near the coatroom almost immediately.

"Ah, you must be Duncan Reed." A tall brunette dressed in a skirt and blouse held out her hand. "My name is Paulina. The director told me to expect you."

Duncan took her hand and shook. "It's lovely to meet you, Paulina. This is my brother, Andy."

She took Andy's hand. "Let me get your coats for you. Take as much time as you need. We're honored to have you back, Mr. Reed."

Duncan nodded as Andy said, "Thank you, miss."

She walked away with their jackets. "The lines you connected on the map create clusters in certain cities," Duncan said. "I believe those cities may be the locations where the remaining groups of Fu Haizi children are held."

"Hot spots. I knew they meant something."

"Yes, the high traffic areas. One of them is Henderson, Nevada."

"Never heard of it," Andy told him as they meandered through the wide entrance of the museum.

"Henderson is just outside Las Vegas. We have a trip planned there just as soon as we complete the search of the Monticello home."

Andy stopped and held out an arm in front of Duncan. "Whoa, brother. That's your shit hanging on the walls."

"I'm hoping it's not shit, but yes. This show is singularly my work. Which means we needed to use my personal pieces. I generally don't mention it to Nickie."

"That's her." Andy pointed to a four-by-eight portrait of Nickie in a full-length ivory gown.

"Ironically, that's the dress I purchased for her during our undercover operation in Las Vegas. The one that stemmed from the discovery of the Henderson location. Now you see why I didn't mention it to her."

Duncan was hoping for more of a quick browse through the museum, but Andy strolled as if he was taking a guided tour.

"Road trips?" Andy asked as he studied a landscape Duncan had painted of the black creek that flowed behind their childhood home.

"Yes." Duncan nodded. "One step at a time, but I'd like to explore each location."

Andy stopped and turned to Duncan as if he'd had an epiphany. "I want in on the search of Nickie's parents' home."

Him and everyone else. "It's too dangerous."

Andy punched him in the shoulder. His brother had arms the size of Duncan's thighs. "What—" He rubbed the spot. "—was that for?"

"For treating me like a girl."

Duncan sighed and circled around to the next area. "Or maybe the father of my nephew. The danger is real. The FBI is involved."

Andy's feet shuffled to a stop. "For real? The FBI?"

Duncan nodded.

"Now I'm really going with you."

CHAPTER 14

No windows in here, but since the interrogation rooms were all on the top floor of the station, Nickie heard thrumming on the ceiling and knew it was still raining. She held out her hand as she walked toward the small metal table in the center of the otherwise empty room. "Dr. Li. Welcome back to Northridge."

Dr. Li stood, the bare feet of her chair scraping against the concrete floor. "Hello, Detective. It's good to be back." She took Nickie's hand and shook twice before gesturing to the only other chair. "Shall we?"

This was Nickie's interrogation room. Role reversal was a bitch. She nodded and sat, folding her hands on the table.

Dr. Li sat as well. Her shiny black hair bobbed as she scooted her chair beneath her. Sitting face-to-face with the doc didn't make her appear as short as she was.

Centered in front of her was a large yellow notepad. Nickie appreciated the old school method of note taking. Lying next to the notepad in three neat piles were papers and file folders. Nickie's papers. Nickie's files. No, she didn't like to share and did not appreciate the intrusion.

"I'd like to start with the mole at the station, if you don't mind," Dr. Li said, flipping through pile number one.

Get this over with, Nick. "Eddy Lynx. Emails sent from

both his work computer and a laptop inadvertently discovered in his home contain email messages, some of which were delivered to computers owned by a Leslie Jacobsen. Email messages about me personally. Times I interrogated Jun Zheng when he was in county."

Dr. Li held up a single pink manicured finger as she wrote in some sort of shorthand Nickie didn't recognize. Nickie raised her brows.

Lowering the finger, Dr. Li tilted her head and lifted her gaze. "First of all, please call me Traci. Second of all, I've had time to read and study your reports. You're thorough and professional. I'm impressed. You don't insert your opinion or verbiage that might be considered subjective in a court of law. No feeling or gut instinct. No wonder you have such an amazing track record." She ended with a warm smile.

Nickie squinted her eyes. Was she trying to suck up?

"I'm not trying to suck up, Detective. Simply stating my observations."

Whoa. Do profilers read minds, too? "Okay. Well, call me Nickie. Or Nick. What can I do to help you, then?"

"I mentioned the former because this is going to make you uncomfortable. As I said, I've read the reports already. Regarding this interview, I'm looking for information about the mole that you would consider personal."

Nickie held up her hands. "Whoa—"

"No, no, Nickie. I don't mean that kind of personal. Although, I must say…interesting."

Great. Nickie just shared her years ago single night with Lynx without sharing it.

"What is he like as a partner? What does his home life look like? Family? Friends? It will help me piece together probable avenues he might be using at this time that may lead to his whereabouts or future plans."

The doc had a proven track record, too. Nickie would give her that. Nodding, Nickie started. "I have to be honest with you, Traci. He wasn't a sharer. Now that I think about it, he was sort of a recluse. I didn't think to nose into his personal life, because I never suspected him of anything. I don't know of any family or friends outside of the station. He gave me shit about my husband. Gave my husband even more shit. He flirted with everyone. Would have bagged the ADA in a heartbeat."

Opening her eyes wide, Traci pulled her chin back.

"Is that subjective enough for ya?"

"It is, yes." Traci smiled again.

"He started acting weird a few weeks ago. Maybe months. I'm not sure. Again, I wasn't looking for it, and I've been kind of busy, you know?"

"You made no mention of this in your report."

"Subjective."

"Right. Of course. Please continue."

She did. Avoiding their single night of misjudgment, she covered his behavior chronologically. The recent times he was MIA or declined coming with her on a case. She ended with the search of his place.

Traci scribbled like mad, filling up a fourth sheet of the oversized lined paper with her secret scribbles, then flipping the page to a clean sheet. She looked up and took a deep breath. Centered along the top, in regular ole English letters, she wrote, Edward Monticello.

Great. Her day was just getting better and better. She waited for the question, but Traci just looked at her with that friendly smile. It wasn't like she didn't know that Nickie saw what she wrote.

"Your father is involved in nearly each piece."

"Yes." At least she didn't avoid calling him Nickie's father.

Never taking her eyes from Nickie, she set her pen down and leaned back in her chair. Nickie couldn't decide if the smile was comforting or creepy. "You have vast experience with pedophiles."

"Vast experience? Is that what we call it these days? I was kidnapped. Raped. Forced to sell myself, to do things that made my parents disown me." Her brows lowered enough to make her eyes close tight. "That's not true. I thought it was." She took a deep breath. "I thought it was the reason they painted the rich-runaway story. Why they gave me up as a ward of the state. I guess that was all a lie. They were covering for what they did. They gave me to Zheng. Got rid of the witness." Lids half opened, she looked up to Traci. "They never expected me to escape. No one ever escapes."

"Would you like something to drink? A break, Detective?"

"Hey. This is my interrogation room. I'm supposed to ask you that."

"You're being funny."

"Yes. Some profiler you are."

"I mean you're discussing tragic childhood memories, some that have come to fruition as we sit here. I'm surprised at your sarcasm, that's all. It takes a lot to surprise me."

Nickie shrugged. "It's a defense mechanism, I suppose. Laugh or cry. It is confusing, I'll tell ya. Yes, I have experience with pedophiles. They come in all shapes and sizes and from all socio and economic statuses. My father is not a pedophile."

Traci squinted.

"You can doubt me all you want. Think I can't possibly see clearly since he is my father and all that. But I'm telling you, he never laid a hand on me. Not aggressively or…" Nickie shivered. "He never showed the signs." It was Nickie's turn to lean back in the chair. "He needed me out of the picture. He owed Zheng money or a favor and got him to abduct me. I find these types run in similar circles. The criminal types, I mean."

Her blood ran cold. The interview was wearing on her. Traci's phone rang. Just in time.

"I need to take this," Traci said and spoke Chinese into it. Nickie gave herself a reprieve and imagined when Eddy would show his ugly face. And he would show, even if she had to wait until she took down Jun Zheng.

"Please forgive me, Nickie," Traci said as she disconnected.

"No worries. Where were we?"

Her phone rang again. Nickie tried to remember where she had been in her lovely kick-Eddy's-ass daydream. But the ring was constant and incredibly obnoxious. And Traci wasn't answering it. Instead, she looked at Nickie with brows lifted high. "Are you going to get that, Detective?"

Oh, it was Nickie's phone. "What the hell," she said as she took it out of her jacket pocket. It wasn't a ring or text tone she recognized. A message flashed across the screen. *ALARM COMPROMISED...ALARM COMPROMISED...*

Traci sat as Nickie tried to get the awful noise to stop. A simple swipe didn't do it and automatically opened an app for her house alarm system. "Sorry, Traci. It's my damned—" She never knew how to work the frigging alarm thing.

On her screen was a photo of nothing. Gray. At the bottom, it read, SW CORNER GARAGE. Her legs stood without her telling them to.

The app flipped to the next view. Gray again. NW CORNER. The system could be wonky, but life experiences taught Nickie to plan for the worst. "It's my home alarm system. I need to...wait—"

The app rotated to the next camera. This one was not gray. The only part of her body that moved was her lungs. This shot was from the camera attached to the third floor of the house. A video of a steady rain coming down in the woods in the back of her house. In the middle of the trees stood a man. She'd know that damned profile anywhere.

Without taking her eyes from her phone, she spun on the balls of her feet and marched out of Interrogation 1. Just before the app rotated to the next screen shot, the monitor blinked, then went to the gray.

...ALARM COMPROMISED...ALARM COMPROMISED...

Oh, hell. She'd already swiped her phone. Now, what did she do? As her phone screeched, she told her feet what to do this time. She told them to run. She started dialing Dave's cell before she realized the sound of expensive pumps followed her.

The ADA spoke from behind. "That's a house alarm notification."

"You know that?" Nickie asked between breaths. "Call for backup."

"You sure it's not a—never mind," said Miranda. "I'll call from the car. I'm going with you."

"If you can keep up," Nickie said, bursting open the door to the stairwell then taking the stairs two at a time.

That damned Eddy Lynx would pay for this. Duncan was out of town. She doubted it was a coincidence. But to break into her house in broad daylight? Or at least broad cloudy, rainy daylight? For what? His computers? They may have been partners at one time, even friends, but he couldn't have known she'd confiscated both his laptop and work computers. And that they were at her place.

"I'll strangle him," Nickie said as she opened the ground floor door to the staff parking area. "I'll strangle him with my own hands."

"Who?" Miranda asked.

She'd kept up? She wasn't even breathing hard from the run down four flights of stairs in those shoes.

"Eddy Lynx." Together, they sprinted to Nickie's ancient Cadillac Eldorado. "I saw him on the visual feed from my home security system. He's shooting out my cameras."

Miranda grabbed the door, slid into the passenger seat and was belted before Nickie had a chance to start the car. "You have security cameras at your house?"

Nickie shifted into reverse and spun the tires on the gravel. "You have no idea," she said as she dropped the gear into forward and spun them again on the way out of the lot.

She barely had time to flip on the siren and lights of her unmarked before the screeching from her phone stopped. The relief was short-lived as the silence was quickly followed by her ring tone. Assuming it had to be Duncan, she initiated her hands-free. Caller ID spoke to her. "Call from Captain Dave Nolan."

"Take the call," she said to the system. "Savage."

"What the hell, Nick? Dr. Li says an alarm went off on your phone and you ran out of here like a bat out of hell." Dave sounded out of breath.

"That bastard Eddy Lynx is at my place shooting out my security cameras. Probably breaking into my house as we speak."

Another call interrupted the one with her captain, but she dared not take it.

"Don't do anything until backup arrives," Dave barked. "I'm calling out the force as soon as we hang up." There was a short pause. Too short to allow Nickie a chance to argue before he added, "That's an order."

The force? As in the whole force? She glanced over at Miranda. Even her prim and proper, by-the-book face said he had to be kidding. "Yeah, okay," Nickie said before disconnecting and speaking into her hands free, "Check voicemail."

"Checking voicemail." Nickie tapped the wheel with her thumb. A muffled voice spoke. "There are five of them. Bring backup."

The voice was unrecognizable.

"Call Duncan Reed," she said to the device.

"Calling Duncan Reed." He didn't answer. In fact, it rang ten times before his voicemail picked up.

"Why aren't you picking up?" She wasn't sure how to break this to him. If the roles were reversed and she was out of town, she would go nuts. The house he had built specifically for them—twice—was under attack and he could do nothing about it when he was over an hour away.

Disconnecting, she gripped the steering wheel tighter and fishtailed on the wet pavement around the last corner. The highway leading to her house was a straightaway and allowed Nickie to open the engines of her old girl. "Come on, baby, don't fail me now."

She flipped off the lights and siren a few miles before her driveway. The damned phone rang again. "Call from, Nevaeh Thornton." Voicemail would have to get that one. Nickie remained silent as she ignored it.

From her peripheral vision, she could see Miranda crane her chin toward her. "Are you going to get that?"

Lifting a single brow, Nickie said, "I'm kinda busy."

"Well, of course. But, it's Nevaeh."

"Holy shit, Miranda. My house is being broken into." Nevaeh was important, yes. But, there wasn't anything Nevaeh had to say that couldn't wait. "By the mole that's been stabbing me in the back for weeks, maybe months. Hell, maybe even years." She was yelling now. Taking it out on the ADA, she knew. "Unless she leaves a message about meeting someone with a falcon tattooed on their arm, there is nothing she has to say that takes precedence right now."

Nickie noticed as the tips of Miranda's fingers curled around her thighs and dug into her pink skirt. Instinctively, she lifted her foot from the gas pedal. The expression on Miranda's face made her think of a deer stuck in headlights. "You okay?"

"Did...Did you say falcon tattoo?"

"Yeah," she answered. "Like the one we saw on Phil the barber? As he lay on the medical examiner's table?"

Miranda shook her head. "I never looked at Phil once the ME pulled the sheets from him. It's Dale. Holy shit, it's Dale," Miranda yelled at the top of her lungs and shook her hands like they were on fire. She grabbed the sides of her perfect hair and took hold.

Nickie raised her voice. "What's Dale?" she asked and slowed down. She thought about taking the back way. She could use the drive leading to her brother-in-law's place, then the lane connecting it to her house. Oh shit, her brother-in-law. "Call Andy Reed," she said to her hands-free. It rang once before it went to voicemail.

"This is Andy with Reed Building and Construction. Leave a message, and I'll call you later."

"Andy, it's Nickie. If you're not home, don't go home. If you are home, don't..." No, that might make him decide to investigate. "Damn it, Andy! Just stay away from my place, okay? Please!"

She hung up and said, "Call Rose Reed."

As it rang, Miranda started yelling again. "It's Dale! Nickie are you listening to me? It's Dale!" Miranda reached and disconnected the call manually.

"What the hell, Miranda? What's the matter with you? What's Parker?"

"He's the mole!" Miranda screamed.

What? "What did you say?"

Miranda grabbed hold of Nickie's right forearm and squeezed. "Oh Nickie, I'm so sorry. I didn't know. You have to believe me."

"You…didn't…know…what?"

"A tattoo of a falcon. Dale has a tattoo of a falcon on his forearm."

How could that be? Nickie's mind spun in a thousand directions as she turned onto Andy's drive. Rain pounded the thick metal top of her ancient vehicle. She could see the Reed Ranch ahead.

Officer Dale Parker. Oh hell, that made sense. He was young. By the books. Under the radar. He came on the scene at the station at the right time. "What have I done?" Nickie said.

Andy and Rose's house was dark. No vehicles could be seen other than excavation equipment and the ones they used for hauling horses. "Call Rose Reed," Nickie growled. "Rose, this is Nickie. Please don't go home until you hear from me, and call that headstrong husband of yours and make sure he doesn't either."

The rain faded to a distant sound. Everything came into focus, if only for her. As if the sheets of water that fell on her windshield cleared the way that she needed to go. Just before her house was visible, she pulled over and shifted into park.

"You wait here," she said to Miranda. "There's no concrete where I'm going. Those heels will sink in the mud. I'll leave my phone with you."

"I'm afraid I'm not comfortable with that," Miranda said.

"No," Nickie said. "You need to stay in touch with backup. Dave is going to be pissed off when he learns I disobeyed a direct order."

She opened her door to the heavy rain. Through the pounding around her, she heard Miranda. "As if he doesn't already know that."

Dipping into the ditch, a stream of warm water ran over the ankles of her leather boots. As she crept closer, the distinct sound of a barking dog became clear. Xena.

Her shoulders stiffened, and her legs bolted. As fast as she could, she pulled out her Smith and Wesson, took it off safety and let the barrel lead the way. If he hurt one hair on Xena's body, he would regret the day he was born.

Her hair stuck to her forehead and neck. Her boots squished in the summer rain. As the house came into view, she noted it seemed intact. No smoke. Her eyes went from one security camera to another. Perfectly centered sniper shots had taken out the glass of each. When did Eddy get to be that good of a shot? The French doors leading from the deck to the house were open. Rain poured into the kitchen.

Where was Duncan? His phone had to have done the same freak out alarm thing hers had done. The fact that he wasn't answering when this shit was happening was making her mind wander to worst-case scenarios.

Movement. In the trees. He wasn't alone.

The random voicemail. It said there were five of them. Who was that? Was it a trap?

Xena's barking was constant and manic. Nickie hadn't heard her sound like this. The bars of her crate banged and clinked.

Nickie pressed flat against one of the bigger tree trunks and let the idea of a long-range rifle aimed at her head pass before she chickened out. Since the trunk wasn't wide enough to cover her, she ducked and zigzagged her way closer.

She spotted three of them. Dressed in black. Running to the next tree, she paused and aimed. The kickback pressed against her locked elbow. It was a needed release even though she missed. Three heads with black skullcaps ducked behind trees.

Her eyes squeezed shut as bullets whizzed past her. One was close enough to brush her hair. She waited as the first round dissipated, then went low, letting off a set of rounds as she rolled in the mush.

CHAPTER 15

A pparently, his brother didn't care to fight the rain this time. As they jogged to Duncan's car, Andy flipped the neck of his coat up over his head. Duncan opened his umbrella and used his remote access to unlock the Jag for him. Deep puddles formed in the landscaping at each corner of the parking lot. The soil would not absorb much more water.

"I think we should try the closer spots first," Andy yelled over the sound of the rain.

"Agreed," Duncan said. He slipped in and said, "Except I plan to investigate Henderson, Nevada, before that. Nickie will want to inspect that site before working with the closer locations."

"I'm looking at this like a bull's-eye covering the country with the center in upstate New York," Andy said before sinking into his side of the car.

Duncan started the Jag.

"Let's start in the center and work our way out," Andy said.

But, Duncan wasn't listening. He'd left his phone on the charger and vividly remembered turning the sound down.

"Hey, loser," Andy asked as he looked around for the source of the piercing sound. "Did you set off the alarm in your car?"

Panic threatening to consume him, Duncan shook his head and grabbed his phone. "No, that is the home security alarm on my phone." Digging into the alarm program, he scanned the video feed as fast as possible, starting from the time the alarm was first triggered. Twenty minutes ago? "Damn it," he yelled. As his heart went from zero to one-twenty in seconds, he threw the car into gear and bolted out of the parking spot. "Damn it, damn it, damn it!" It would take over an hour to get home going the speed limit. He pressed the gas pedal to the floor and fishtailed onto the highway.

His knuckles turned white as he gripped the steering wheel. His brother didn't comment about the speed reaching over one hundred miles per hour. Duncan's senses were zoned on the police scanner he had rigged to pick up the private NPD channel. It seemed as if there was little chance of getting a ticket as all squads were headed for his home.

"The alarm has been compromised," Duncan growled to Andy. "Your home is too close to mine. Call Rose and tell her to stay away until we contact her."

Andy clicked his seat belt into place and nodded. "Get us there in one piece, brother. Rose is at work."

"Call her anyway. Eddy Lynx is behind this. Pouring rain or not, I recognize him from the still shots my security alarm took in my backyard. He finally grew the balls to show his face. If he touches my dog, I'm going to kill him."

"Hey, now," Andy said over the rain. "We're not going to be killing anyone today. What if you got there—?"

"Detective Eddy Lynx," Duncan said. "Did you hear me? That was Lynx's ugly face that showed in my backyard."

He woke the hands-free device installed in his Jaguar. "Call my wife." Relief flooded him as it was answered after the first ring. The relief was short-lived as the voice on the other end was not his Nickie.

"Duncan? This is Assistant District Attorney Miranda Vaughn."

"Where is she?" He knew the answer to that question before he'd finished speaking. It was difficult to hear her between the sound of the pounding rain and the pounding in his head.

"Your alarm has been compromised," Miranda yelled. "I'm in the car. Nickie is investigating. Backup is on the way."

Thirty minutes left. If he went any faster, they wouldn't make it there alive.

"Nickie told me to man the phones, mostly for your call. Now, you've called, so I'm going to help her."

"Are you alone?" he asked.

"Yes. I am digging out a pair of Nickie's boots from her backseat. There. All better. Gotta go."

She sounded much too driven with the idea. This was not her expertise, nor her training. But at that moment, all he cared about was his wife. "Bring her phone with you. Turn off the ringer. Make sure the vibration feature is still activated."

"I will. Officer Dale Parker is a motherfucker."

The line disconnected. Officer Parker? Surely, Miranda didn't intend to add in a trivial piece of office drama at a time like this. He needed to get back.

The saplings that swayed in the blowing wind made it difficult to tell which were trees and which were people. Every few seconds, Nickie saw an unmistakable body dressed in black darting between them. The noise from her footsteps sloshing in the muddy leaves was muted by the sound of the storm. Flashes of lightning were rare through the dense trees, but gave occasional glimpses of the outlines of the men.

Jun Zheng's men. Eddy Lynx. Officer Parker. Her blood boiled, the water running down her back doing little to cool her off. Two other men in mock turtlenecks and skullcaps strolled out through her back door. Hadn't they heard the shootout?

They held Eddy's laptop and his computer from work. She'd left them out in the open, sitting on the desk in her master bedroom. Nickie thought she might have even left them on. Neither of the men was Eddy Lynx or Officer Parker.

She stood tall, hiding behind as much of the skinny trunk as she could. Using a branch to steady her arm, she aimed, but it wasn't at the two on the deck.

One of them stepped out from his cover. "Get down!" yelled a deep voice. "We've been made!"

There it was. Aiming toward the voice, she emptied the magazine on her Smith and Wesson. "Umph," the voice grunted. Nickie watched as the figure leaned his back against a tree and slid down. Her adrenaline spiked and her fingers trembled. Not a kill shot. But it would do.

Simultaneously, she ducked and released the empty magazine onto the wet ground. A slew of bullets buzzed past her head. The adrenaline flowed fast enough that she almost didn't notice the one that grazed her arm. "Shit," she said too loudly. Flesh wound. "I really liked this jacket," she grumbled and shoved a new clip into her Smith and Wesson.

Rolling onto the wet leaves, Nickie stopped on her stomach, aimed and emptied her next magazine. She alternated between the two men who carried Eddy's equipment and the ones in the trees. Two down this time. One got up and hobbled away. One didn't. Another clip out, another in. Only one spare to go.

The distant sound of sirens became evident. Loads of them. The perps must have heard them, too, as they scattered like cockroaches in light.

Before she could take advantage of the dispersing and unload another round, Nickie heard a female voice from behind her. "Don't shoot. It's me, Miranda."

"What the hell," Nickie said, not at all trying to be quiet. "Are you trying to get yourself killed?" Glancing over her shoulder, Nickie saw a pink skirt slithering over the wet ground. It was some kind of imitation army crawl. Except the ADA's butt stuck up making it a pink target.

"Give me a gun," Miranda whispered, using her elbows to pull herself through the leaves.

The men were long gone. Well, all except the two down, but Nickie reached and handed her the Glock from her pant leg anyway.

Her house had not been blown up. Nothing was on fire. When did she get to the place in her life where this was a good thing?

The sound of screeching tires and more sirens than she could count sounded from the front of the house. Had Dave ordered every available officer on duty? Of course, he did. He would do it for any cop who had their home infiltrated by an escaped fugitive and murderer. He may have called in the off-duty patrols as well.

The perp against the tree was a problem. He might still have the site of his gun aimed their way. As dozens of feet stomped around her house, she crept on her stomach, focusing on the lifeless shape lying in the mud. Miranda followed at her heels.

She didn't recognize the man. He lay unnaturally on his side with an arm craned behind him. Digging her fingers beneath his jawbone, she felt for a pulse. Nothing. She readjusted the position of her fingers. Still nothing.

Before moving on, she glanced at Miranda. Wide-eyed, the ADA's hand covered her mouth as she stared at the dead perp.

"It's not like you've never seen a dead body before."

"Yes. Yes, you're right. Just not one that was warm."

Eww. Now, Nickie was thinking about it, and she didn't want to think about it. She wanted to get to the injured perp and then inside to check on her home and to let Xena out before the girl bit through the bars of her crate.

"Detective Savage," a familiar voice yelled from about twenty yards ahead. A back-stabbing ballsy bastard familiar voice. "It's me, Officer Parker. I've got him, sir. I've got Lynx subdued."

Miranda's fingers wrapped around Nickie's calf and squeezed.

He's got him? This should be interesting. Nickie ignored the sound of feet coming from both sides of the house.

"You stay here," she said to Miranda. "I mean it. I'll shoot you, too, if you move a damned muscle and ruin this." Nickie stood tall and walked toward Parker, her gun at her side. Against protocol, she held her finger over the trigger.

"The rest got away, sir. Except the one you capped. Nice job, by the way."

As she got closer, she noted it was Parker who she'd shot. He was in full uniform, hat and all. A ring of bright red blood circled a small hole in the shoulder of his police-issue jacket. He held the injured arm close to his body. With the other, he pointed the barrel of his gun into Eddy's temple.

Parker had Eddy on his knees, hands clasped behind his head. No matter how much she didn't like either of them, Nickie did her best to ignore the gun dug into her partner's temple. She nodded to Parker. How could she not have known? Turning to Eddy, she said, "There you are, Lynx. Long time no see."

Lynx looked her in the eye, expanded his lungs, then released the air slowly.

"Roll up your sleeves," she said to Lynx but focused on Officer Parker.

Parker's eyes grew bigger. It was only for a split second before he dropped them down to half closed, but she didn't miss it. He knew why she was asking and shoved the gun deeper into Eddy's temple. "You heard the detective," he said. "Roll up your sleeves."

Eddy squinted his eyes at her. He was definitely confused, but seemed to know where she was going with this, too. She didn't want to believe it. She wanted this to be all Parker, but she had to know. Had to see. She just did.

Without speaking, Eddy answered the call of the barrel shoved in his temple. "There are five of them," he said as he did as they'd asked. The words on the voicemail. "Did you bring backup?" He rotated his forearms, showing the bare fronts and backs.

From head to toe, a tsunami of relief flooded through her. She moved her eyes to Parker. He seemed to relax at the fact that she wasn't asking him to do the same, but she didn't need to ask him to expose his arms. She already had Miranda's eyewitness testimony.

The sound of her captain's voice thundering through a bullhorn came from the west side of the house. Dave brought a bullhorn? "This is Captain Dave Nolan from the Northridge Police Department. Drop your weapons and come out with your hands clasped behind your heads."

"It's Officer Parker, sir," Parker yelled. "I'm here with Detective Savage. We've shot one of the intruders dead, and have Detective Lynx apprehended."

Nickie eyeballed the gun pressed into her partner's temple. Sticking her hand behind her back, she crooked a finger at Miranda. She stared at Parker and tilted her head. Miranda—soaking wet and covered in muddy leaves—marched up to Parker, pulled her elbow back and punched him in the center of his face. It was the lamest, wimpiest punch Nickie had ever seen. But apparently she'd landed it, because Nickie heard a crunch followed by a wail from Parker.

"What the fuck? You broke my nose!"

Miranda shook her hand as if her pitiful, wimpy punch had broken her knuckles. But then, she pulled back for another.

Eddy lifted both brows. "Impressive," he said, then released his hands from behind his head, holding them out in surrender. Nickie grabbed Miranda's arm before she really hurt herself. Eddy looked to Nickie. Nickie winked at him. Eddy's eyes widened, then his face relaxed with understanding.

Quick as hell, he swiped the gun out of Parker's good hand and punched him in the side of his face damned rock-solid hard. Parker swayed and fell backward, knocked out like a light. The bigger they are, the harder they fall, and Parker fell with a splash. Still holding the barrel of Parker's gun, Eddy held it out to Nickie, his other arm lifted high.

She took it from Eddy before someone got the wrong idea and shot him. They stared at each other for a long moment. Searchlights circled them. In the spotlight, he kept his gaze on hers and turned his chin to the side. "You know," he said. "you really have Xena trained well."

Her dog? What? But before she could ask Eddy what he meant, Miranda fell on the unconscious Dale Parker. She wailed as she unbuttoned the cuffs of Parker's limp left arm. Grabbing hold of his wrist, she shoved up the sleeve. "This!" she said, exposing the falcon tattoo, then pounded on his chest with the sides of her fists.

Eddy shrugged and Nickie lifted a brow but decided Miranda deserved her moment. As the ADA got out her issues, Dave came into Nickie's line of vision. He stood next to Eddy and seemed to understand.

"I knew you wouldn't believe me," Eddy said. "The setup had been too good. My computer at work, tricking me into getting Jun Zheng out that day. I wasn't alone. Zheng wasn't the one who shot me. It was the motherfucker currently getting a beating from the girl in a dirty pink skirt."

They looked down at the scene as Miranda's anger turned to tears.

"Hell hath no fury like a pissed off woman," Eddy said. It was close enough to the proverb and made Nickie laugh. Poor Miranda.

"Come now," Nickie said and took her arm. Pulling gently, she realized Miranda was stronger than a girl in a dirty pink skirt should—hey! Those were Nickie's favorite riding boots, muddy and on the ADA's feet. Pulling not at all gently, she hauled the scorned woman from Officer Parker and yelled toward the house where Xena continued her crazed barking. "Someone let out my dog, would you?"

Searchlights exposed a dozen faces she recognized and some she didn't. Yes, Dave must have brought every available police officer out to her place. He was one of the best people she had in her life.

The men looked at each other. A few glanced at the house, shook their heads and glanced back at Nickie.

"Oh, grow a pair already. She's a pup." Nickie turned back to Lynx. "I'm really glad you're not a backstabbing bastard." He leaned in and nuzzled his nose against her ear. She rolled her eyes and pulled away from him. Some things never changed.

"And I'm really glad you shot Parker and not me," he said. "My gut still hurts like a motherfucker from the hole he put in me." He reached over and took Miranda's arm. "There, now," he said to her.

She wrapped her arms around him and sobbing, dug her face into his shoulder.

"We'll ride with one of the guys back to the station for debriefing," he said, guiding her through the crowd of officers.

Nickie noticed Xena had stopped barking. She turned to check the house as the girl came tearing out of the open back door and down the deck steps. Her normally clumsy, happy, playful dog bounded over the deck railing and landed ten feet below without a hitch. She rolled like a veteran skydiver, then got up and made a beeline for Officer Parker. Her teeth sank into his thigh, waking him from his unconsciousness.

Eddy spun and said, "Xena, release." The girl obeyed and trotted over, then sat near Eddy's leg. What the hell? Xena whined and nuzzled his pants.

Dave lunged at Parker. Not that there was much Parker could do with a gunshot wound, a broken nose and a dog bite. Nonetheless, Dave rolled him on his stomach, stuck a knee in the center of his back and cuffed him.

"I told you," Eddy said. "You trained her well." He released Miranda and squatted down, letting Xena cover his face with slobber. "There you are, good girl. That's right. You're a good dog."

Dave's phone rang. "Captain Nolan," he said into his cell.

Eddy looked at Nickie. "You should check your video feed more often. She and I have been getting to be good friends." He scratched her on the top of her head. "You took my black glove, girl. Didn't you?"

"You," Dave yelled as he pointed to two officers. "Secure the house. This is all a diversion. The station has been breached."

CHAPTER 16

The police scanner interrupted the growl of the engine and patter of the rain that fell around Duncan. Gripping the shaking steering wheel, he wasn't sure if it trembled from the speed or the battle going on in his head. As his fingers dug in, his mind carried out a silent debate. He worked to convince himself that the police scanner was a police scanner. It had been a simple device to manipulate. He'd done it in order to infiltrate the NPD secure channel. It was not—with a mental emphasis on the word not—the radio in the Chinook he rode during his stint in the Middle East. The rain was rain. Water coming from the sky and pelting his car. It was not a torrent of bullets coming at his platoon, hitting the metal of his helicopter. At least the steady 110 mph cut travel time nearly in half.

Nickie hadn't answered her phone. Duncan assumed the ADA had left it in Nickie's car. Short audio clips from the walkies over the scanner confirmed the alarm notification on his phone. The communication between Captain Nolan and the others told him Xena was unharmed and his home was secure. The criminals were apprehended, and his Nickie was safe.

"There's been a breach at the station." It was the captain's voice yelling in the walkie onto said secure channel. "This was a diversion. I repeat. This was a diversion." The news erased any issues of reality and sucked Duncan back into the present danger. "The profiler has confirmed shots fired. Says she's well-hidden on the top floor."

Safe, yet used as a diversion?

Before he could change his mind, Duncan said mostly to himself, "To the station."

"Are you sure you don't want to stop and check out your place?" his brother yelled over the noise as they passed the highway that led to their homes. Duncan had been so focused on fighting the flashback he'd almost forgotten that Andy sat next to him in the passenger seat.

Static cleared from the scanner. Duncan listened as the captain yelled, "All black and whites with the exception of numbers nine and fourteen get to the station. Go now. I'm right behind you."

"I'm sure," Duncan answered Andy. "We're almost there now." He slowed enough to take the first corner, the tires hugging the pavement, as if they were on rails. "I'll park a few blocks away. I need you to stay here, close to the police scanner, and alert me via text if you hear anything I need to know."

"Nice try, brother. You're not going in alone."

Duncan's mind wandered to his brother's wife and baby. As he veered to the curb three blocks from the station, Andy opened the glove box and pulled out his Glock. "I assume you have your Beretta under your seat."

Under other circumstances, Duncan would have preferred to carry both. "I do."

Duncan opened his door before the vehicle came to a complete stop, yanked on the emergency brake and decided on Andy's trick, lifting the back of his coat over his head. Ignoring the puddles, he jogged through the rain, checking between each building down the street. Empty except for a few cars that drove at normal speeds as if murderers weren't infiltrating the station.

Gun drawn and inside the front of his jacket, Duncan took the staff parking lot door. He walked as if he knew nothing of what transpired inside. He used his copy of Nickie's scan card to get through the employee's only door, then elevator.

As Andy passed the threshold, Duncan pressed the button for the top floor, then reached to the small mirror in the corner. He wrapped his fingers around it and pulled, jerking it from its corner. Knowingly, they each took subsequent sides of the sliding doors, hiding from view when they opened.

"Gun ready?" Duncan asked.

"Yeah, I'm ready." Andy nodded and pulled his gun to his chest.

"When the doors open," Duncan added. "I use the mirror to check for anyone in view. We go in low."

"I'll roll right, you left."

Duncan sighed. "I'm still not comfortable with this."

"You shouldn't be, brother. These guys suck."

A single bell. A roll of the metal doors. Duncan held up the mirror. Nothing moving or standing. Two motionless bodies lay on the floor. Setting the mirror down, he ducked and rolled before the elevator doors shut behind them.

Duncan held up a fist, signaling for Andy to wait. No sound. The office door behind him was open. Pulling himself by his elbows, Duncan checked inside. No feet below. No heads above. He ducked inside and squatted under the light switch. Andy didn't follow, and Duncan could only hope he'd done something similar

No footsteps. No voices. Standing, he glanced through the door. Andy was halfway around the commons area. He was checking each office as he went. It was too fast. Duncan would kick his ass when this was over. Gun drawn, he crept with loose knees toward the first body. It was the new guy. Duncan had only seen him around a few times. No introduction. No name. A bullet between his eyes, the body stared at the ceiling, the look of terror stuck on his face.

Duncan squatted and closed the lids on the young man's eyes. Searing heat ignited his body. And fear. Not fear for his own safety, or even for Andy's at this point. But a fear that they were too late.

Andy had made it to the captain's office. Duncan checked over each shoulder once again before squatting down to the other body. Female. Facedown next to her desk. Heavy. Dressed in a turquoise blue pantsuit. He didn't need to roll her over to know who it was. Lucinda, the nosy desk clerk. Placing his fingers against her carotid, he felt for a pulse. Nothing. As he'd been taught in basic training, he readjusted his fingers and tried again. Still nothing.

Useless death. His brows came together and he placed the palm of his hand against the spot between his eyes. As he shut them, he saw explosions, blood and death. So much death.

"Brother."

Yes. They were brothers for life. Each and every member of his platoon. War did that to you.

"Duncan, it's me. Come on, man. This floor is empty. Let's check the other levels."

Duncan blinked and glanced up. His brother looked down on him. He released the tight grip he didn't realize he had on Lucinda's arm. "No. Traci Li is here somewhere. Dave said this floor," he said, shaking his head clear.

"I didn't find any other bodies. This is bad, man." Andy glanced from the lifeless form of the new guy to Lucinda and back again. "Bad."

Duncan stood and took a breath. "Yes. This seems to get bigger with each move."

"Yeah. Nick's office is a mess."

Turning his head that way, he noticed that the cheap plastic mini blinds were open. Even in the rain, her skinny office windows let in enough light to see the disaster that was her office. The drawers on both of her tall filing cabinets were open. He walked toward the open door to see the floor carpeted with papers. It seemed like everything from the top of her desk had been swept across the floor and each item from the inside was strewn everywhere. Her lamp and printer were shattered. Had they thrown it at the walls? This was more than a search. It was a message.

"Come," Duncan said. "We need to find the profiler." They checked the interrogation rooms. Not many files or items to mess with in there. Except the third one. It was rarely used for interrogation and more of a storage space. It had been ransacked but not as much as Nickie's office had been.

They opened the cracked door of the interrogation observation room. Duncan would have missed her if he hadn't smelled the faint scent of strawberry shampoo. She was small enough that she'd squeezed between the wall and the thin metal plate against the underside of the only desk in the room.

"Traci? It's me, Duncan Reed. I'm—"

"I know who you are," she said. He'd expected fear in her voice, but it wasn't fear he heard.

"This is my brother, Andy."

"We need to call in the FBI. I know no one around here wants to hear that, but this is bigger than any of us expected." Yes. Not fear at all, but anger and plenty of it.

"Where's Detective Savage? Where's Captain Nolan?" she barked as she straightened her skirt and brushed off her blouse.

"They heard your message and are on the way. Are you hurt? Can I get you anything? Water? Something sweet? It will help—"

"What I need is to do my job here. Which involves debriefing, then to continue my interview with your wife." She ran her hands over the top of her hair and stepped into the center of the room. "Followed by filling in the Federal Bureau of Investigation."

"You're going the wrong way, Detective," the ADA said from the passenger seat of Nickie's ancient police issue. As if Nickie didn't know the way around town.

She let her foot sink a little harder on the gas pedal. The sound of the engine soothed the raw nerves that were ready to break. "We're not going to the station. You should have ridden with Eddy."

"It felt like ditching."

"Ditching? Did the proper Assistant District Attorney just say, 'ditching?' And, thanks, by the way."

"My favorite pink suit is covered in mud. I'm wearing motorcycle boots. It's a good time to use the word ditching."

Nickie squealed her tires around the last corner. "Those are not motorcycle boots. To be motorcycle boots, you need either no buckles or many more buckles. Those have two."

"I didn't know there were rules to thi—Oh. I see where you're going."

It killed Nickie not to be at the station, but Duncan had texted her to let her know he was there and her captain had surely joined him by then. Their home, the station. Jun Zheng was looking for something, and the place he would make sure to include in his search would be Duncan's office.

She pulled over to the opposite side of the street and parked.

"Duncan's office is in there," Miranda said.

"Yes. He owns the top floor." Even through the rain, Nickie could see the blinds were open and his office manager sitting at her desk.

Miranda looked out the windshield, then turned around to see out the back. "It's the tallest building in Northridge."

"This and the police station. I don't know that we can say tall for a four-story building, but yeah." Nickie opened the car door and avoided the wide puddles. With the motorcycle boots, Miranda splashed through them.

They entered the building and passed the elderly janitor as he pushed his cart out of the elevator. Nickie stepped aside to let him pass. "Hello, Jimmy. How is your day?"

"Just fine, Mrs. Reed. Just fine."

No hint of distress in his voice. "You have a nice day now."

"Will do, miss. Will do." They traded places, Jimmy exiting the elevator as she and Miranda stepped in.

"He called you Mrs. Reed," she said as the door closed behind them.

Nickie shrugged. "It happens." She pressed the button to the fourth floor.

The other two attacks were simultaneous. This one would have been as well, yet the building appeared intact. She would at the very least send the office manager home for the day.

"If you don't mind me asking, I've been with you through this entire ordeal thus far and you haven't called Duncan."

Lowering her brows, Nickie turned her eyes to her. She couldn't tell the ADA that her husband would be listening to the police scanner he'd hacked and would know everything that was going on. So, like she'd said about Nevaeh. "He texted me, and I'm kinda busy."

Nevaeh. Oh no. She pressed the third floor button, and the elevator jerked to a stop.

"What are we doing?" Miranda asked.

Nickie held up a finger and dialed Duncan's number as the doors opened to the floor below Duncan's offices. She held the open doors button. Voicemail answered after the first ring. She texted Duncan as she left the message, "Duncan, it's me. Nevaeh was due at the station. I'm worried she's a casualty. Please call." She punched the wall.

Miranda looked at her with a mixture of confusion and fear.

"Call the captain," she said to the intel assist in her phone.

"Calling Captain Nolan," it said. No answer. Nickie punched the elevator wall once more, then searched her recent calls, found Nevaeh's and pressed *send*.

"This is Nevaeh. You know what to do."

A third floor passerby walked past the still-open elevator door with wide eyes, staring at the two of them.

"Nevaeh, you call me before you go to the station. That's an order."

Nickie nodded at the strolling stranger, smiled and let go of the open doors button. Pressing the fourth floor several times, she took a deep breath. "I want you to stay in the elevator, Miranda. Get out of sight right here," she said and pressed a hand against the button panel. "If I don't come back in five, call for backup. Black and whites can get here in minutes."

"You want me to stay in the elevator?"

"Yes," Nickie said as she took her gun out of her holster and held it at her side.

She stepped out and headed for the door that had 'Duncan Reed' carved in large wooden letters. With her free hand, she rotated the knob. It turned easily, and she walked into the reception area.

Duncan's office manager looked up and smiled. "Hello, Detective Savage. He is not here."

Nickie briefly scanned her face and noted the strands of sweaty black hair that stuck to the sides.

She nodded. "No worries, Megan." Nickie took a step toward Duncan's office just as she heard something moving under Megan's desk. "I can come back later," she said in an easy voice just before bending her knees and bursting through the air toward the door to Duncan's office. Diving across the area, she scanned the room, then tumbled to the floor and rolled. She landed a step away from Duncan's door. Two of the bastards. One under the office manager's desk and the other behind the door she'd just come through.

She shot one in the thigh as bullets came at her. She rolled once more and got the other perp in the gut as she erupted through to Duncan's office. A quick roll and check of the room told her there were no cowards hiding under his desk or behind the door.

Her house, the station and Duncan's office. Now, she was really pissed off.

CHAPTER 17

With the two incapacitated, Nickie ran back to Megan. Both men howled. The one with a bullet in his thigh thrashed around the office manager's feet. Ignoring Megan's screams, Nickie walked to the thrasher and took his gun from the floor next to him. She did a visual on Number Two as she stuffed Thrasher's gun into the belt at her back. The howls of Number Two were more of a moan as he lay still on the floor.

She unlocked her cell and placed it in front of Megan. "Can you call Captain Nolan?" The office manager stopped screaming when she realized Nickie was talking to her. "Can you call Captain Nolan?" Nickie repeated. Megan grabbed the phone like it might disappear any second and started pecking at the screen. The task would keep her from going into shock if nothing else.

Patting down Thrasher was no easy task. His other gun was in his pant leg. She stuffed it in her belt next to the first one. After rolling him onto his stomach, she pressed a knee into his back.

"You bitch," he yelled as the handcuffs clicked around his wrists.

"Yeah, yeah, yeah. I get that all the time."

She wanted them alive. Needed them alive for questioning. She pulled Thrasher next to Number Two who was bleeding from his side. Since she'd used her cuffs already, she grabbed an extra zip tie from a compartment on her belt and cuffed Number Two's hands in the front, then checked around for something to put pressure on the wound.

"There were two of them. Nickie shot them," Megan yelled into the phone. "Um, yes. An ambulance is needed."

A female scream came from the elevator. Nickie ducked behind the frame of the doorway. Her breath quickened, and her senses went into overdrive. She knew exactly what she'd seen. Jun Zheng held Miranda by the throat, his gun shoved under her chin.

The office manager started screaming again, Nickie's phone still against her ear. With one more scan of the cuffed men and the area around her, Nickie drew her gun, locked her elbows and spun to face her childhood captor.

"My beautiful savage," he crooned. In contrast to Miranda's wide eyes, his were relaxed, a slight smile curving the corners of his lips.

Fire ignited in Nickie's gut, yet seemed to slow down everything around her. Using the barrel of her gun as a scope, she aimed for the spot between his eyes. She didn't need this one alive. They'd already had him in custody for months. He didn't talk then, and he wouldn't talk now.

For a fraction of a second, she imagined pulling the trigger. She could do it. Easy shot really, even with the ADA shaking and gasping in his grip. She could end this all now, end him.

He wore the same getup as the rest of them. Black pants and mock turtleneck. His hair spiked at the forehead like he'd just styled it. No sweat lined his brow. Not like he'd caused on the office manager. He held Miranda with confidence and force. His lips turned into a condescending grin. "Put down your gun before I—"

Nickie dropped her aim and pulled the frigging trigger. She grazed the arm he'd been stupid enough to wrap around the front of Miranda. Zheng spun to his right from the impact, then jerked his gaze to her in disbelief. Before he had a chance to regroup, she pounced forward and pointed her gun to the side of his head.

The ADA screamed again.

The office manager screamed again.

"I really hate it when you call me that," Nickie said to him and dug her gun into his temple.

Zheng opened his fingers, let his gun drop and held up his arms.

"Miranda," Nickie said. From her peripheral vision, she noted the ADA wouldn't be able to hear the way she had her hands pressed to the sides of her head. "Miranda," she yelled this time. Both Miranda and the office manager stopped screaming. While holding his arms up, Zheng darted his gaze around the area. He was looking for his out, and Nickie was determined not to give him one. "Give me a reason, Zheng," she said and pressed the gun against his head a little harder. "Give me a reason."

"Get me a zip tie from the right side of my belt." Miranda stepped behind Nickie. Nickie felt as the snap of her pepper spray compartment opened but refused to take her focus from Zheng. "Other right side," she said.

Miranda held out the tie and Nickie took it with her free hand. "Sorry, Zheng." Not really. "This is going to hurt." Nickie took his good arm, then his bad one and secured them behind his back.

"You—" She pointed to Megan. "—get a wad of paper towels from the bathroom. I need to put pressure on his wound," she said as she gestured her chin toward the perp on the floor with the hole in his side. He'd propped himself up against the wall, but he wasn't going anywhere on his own.

She pulled the zip tie a few extra clicks just because it made her feel good. Yanking Zheng along by his tied hands, she dragged him over next to his buddies and shoved him to the floor a body's length away from them. In the doorway, Megan was back, already holding three rolls of paper towels.

"I've got it," Miranda said. She took the towels from Megan's hand and stepped to the wounded. Nickie lifted her brows as the ADA ripped open his shirt and applied pressure. Maybe she wasn't quite the wuss Nickie thought she was.

Sliding a chair a few yards in front of the three, Nickie sat and huffed out a long breath. "Everything's going to be okay." She pointed the gun toward them as she pulled out her phone.

She glanced at the screen of her cell. Two missed calls. "Shit." She used her speed dial and called the captain.

"Nick," Dave answered. "Backup is on the way. You okay?"

"Yeah. I've got three of them, two wounded. One is Jun Zheng," she said as she cocked her head and squinted at him.

"Are you safe?" Dave asked.

"I am," Nickie said. "We are. I've got the ADA with me. How are things at the station?" she asked.

"It's not good, Nick. Are you sure you're okay?"

"I am. Miranda and—" Nickie turned and whispered in the phone, "—and I'm guessing one soon-to-be-former office manager are not so great."

"That's too bad," he said. "We'll get Miranda some time off after we start the proceedings. Parker's going to make it, but you've got one bagged at the scene at your house. You'll need some time off as well, Nick."

"When hell freezes over."

"Mandatory time, Detective."

"Bureaucratic crap."

Dave ignored that comment. "Duncan wants to talk to you."

Her heart rate instantly slowed. It may have only gone from one twenty beats per minute to a hundred, but Duncan did that for her and she was grateful.

"Nickie?"

"Any signs of Nevaeh?"

"No. We searched every corner for the profiler."

"You found Dr. Li?"

"Yes. She is safe. Nickie, I have something I need to tell you."

"I'm here. I saved your office," she said, adrenaline racing and ignoring his statement.

"I heard, and to hell with my place."

"I know, but I got three alive. We'll need them for questioning. One of them is Zheng."

The pause was too long. She heard running footsteps. "Duncan? Duncan, is everything okay? What about the station? Is anyone hurt?"

"I'm on my way," he said.

His office. Why hadn't he thought of his office? Duncan gripped his steering wheel until his fingers ached. The lights from two ambulances and a pair of squad cars circled the entire downtown area.

From a block away, he could see through the wall of windows into his office space. Several people stood scattered around the area. The scene appeared to be secure.

Without him.

His Nickie. She'd apprehended three perpetrators single-handedly.

Sliding into the spot in front of his office building behind the two squad cars, he pulled the emergency brake and flew out of his car. An additional officer stood huddled with what Duncan recognized as workers from other areas of the building. A few more were guided out the front door by another officer.

Duncan dodged through them and addressed the man in blue leading people to safety. "I am here with—"

"I know who you are," the officer said but didn't step out of the way. Duncan didn't care one way or another and stepped around him.

The elevator doors opened to organized chaos. The first thing his eyes searched for was his Nickie. She stood unharmed, huddled with two officers Duncan had never seen before. A powerful weight lifted from his chest and floated away. He'd known she was okay, but something inside of him must have needed to see it for himself. Knowing what she'd been through, he felt justified.

He slipped out of the elevator and held open the doors for two EMTs pushing a stretcher that carried a man dressed in black pants and mock turtleneck.

Another perpetrator lay on a board as additional EMTs blew up a temporary cast around the length of his leg. This was all consequential since Duncan's eyes were mostly focused on one man. Jun Zheng sat alone on the floor, centered along the wall between Duncan's personal office door and the hallway that led to his set of bathrooms.

The expression on the bastard's face was wrong. Zheng worked far too hard to appear smug. His hands were behind his back, but he sat still, too still, and it took much too long for him to notice as Duncan stepped toward him.

"No," Nickie yelled as Duncan flipped Zheng on his side.

Duncan didn't have time to inspect the handcuffs behind Zheng's back. There weren't any. A neatly cut zip tie hung from the wrist that swung around toward the side of Duncan's head. Duncan ducked enough to dodge most of the blow, but the hook grazed his left brow, jerking his head to the side.

In the fraction of a second it took for Duncan to regain his balance, a pocketknife had materialized in Zheng's hand. He dodged the blade as Zheng swept it across his midsection and the follow-up round-house kick at his head.

Fancy karate shit. He caught Zheng's glare long enough to fake a jab and follow it up by a shoulder-heavy punch to the side of his face. Duncan stepped back as Zheng wavered and the officers swarmed.

Nickie stood with her hands out, suspicion in her eyes. It pained him when she feared him. "I'm me," he said in a language of understanding only the two of them knew. He was he. He was here. No flashback. His mind was not that of a soldier left in the desert pulling the bodies of his platoon from his Chinook. Unfortunately, he understood why she needed to be sure.

She nodded and took his hand as she turned to inspect the altercation between Zheng and the officers. One used handcuffs to secure his arms behind his back as the other pulled out a set of leg shackles. Together, they hoisted him to his feet and yanked him upright.

Blood dripped from his smiling mouth as Zheng's gaze dropped to Duncan's and Nickie's joined hands. Duncan tried to release their connection, but Nickie squeezed tighter. "Karma's a bitch, Zheng. I'm bringing you to the station myself. Your minion won't get you out this time."

The station. Duncan dipped his lips close to her ear. "I need to tell you something. It's about the station."

It was like she'd been up for days. The weight of the scene pulled Nickie's shoulders down as she stood over the body. Lucinda. Shot as she sat at her cheap metal desk, working at a job that paid her little to nothing.

The coroner was done, and he had moved to the new dude lying lifeless on the other side of the commons area. Which made it Nickie's job to give the nod to bag her. She'd photographed every angle. Recorded the details on her old school recorder. Then, why couldn't she say the words?

The mess that was her office would be nothing compared to this. Single gunshot between the eyes. Kill shot. Lucinda was likely dead before she slid out of her office chair and hit the floor. She had grown kids and a husband.

The backs of Nickie's eyes burned and threatened to betray her. A strong hand covered the top of her shoulder. Her captain. She glanced to the other side of the room. Chocolate brown eyes of support watched her as Duncan nodded slightly enough that only she would see it.

Nickie inhaled deeply, then told the men patiently waiting, "Bag her." Her voice caught, but she had to be strong for the countless girls that needed to be saved from all this. That Lucinda died for in the process. "Take her downstairs. The ME will get to her when he can." When he could. He had four bodies from here and one from Duncan and Nickie's house.

This was the Northridge Police Department. Rickard's lab didn't have room for five bodies, let alone any down there who died from natural causes since his lab doubled as the temporary city morgue. Was that where Nickie just sent Lucinda? To a metal drawer to wait her turn? She'd worked at the station long before Nickie was transferred here. Now, she was dead because of people who wanted Nickie dead.

And why hadn't they taken a shot at Nickie, she wondered as she skipped her office and turned for the captain's. They obviously had plenty of men. The operation was big enough, deep enough, extensive enough.

Her father was part of this organization. Did he have a tattoo of a falcon on his left forearm? Or did Jun Zheng let the one inlaid in his foyer suffice?

There were extra guest chairs in Dave's office. It made her stop short and wonder where they came from. As if that mattered in any way, shape or form.

Dave followed her in and sat in his enormous chair behind his desk. In the chairs were Miranda, Eddy, Duncan and Andy. In that order. With the chair right in the middle empty. Head spinning, she sank down.

"I'm sorry that took so long. The two security officers downstairs at the screening station were found in an adjacent room. Single gunshots to the forehead. Same with the desk clerk, who sits…who sat just outside my office. It looks like the new guy was shot by someone else. His was a chest shot. Sloppier."

CHAPTER 18

Nickie closed her eyes before continuing. "No one on floors two or three seemed to know anything was amiss. They are no worse for the wear." She sighed, her lids refusing to open. "Cameras say there were nine of them."

Nine. She shook her head. At least five at her house. Three at Duncan's office. That was seventeen. Yes, why didn't they just kill her and get it over with?

"It appears they came in, took out security, then stood guard at the two entrance doors. Witnesses say a man in a white jumpsuit turned them away when they tried to enter the facility. Told them there was a gas leak. By the time social media spread the word around, Zheng's men were gone.

"They went right for my office, Dave. And Eddy's. That and the break-ins at my place…at Duncan's office, they lead toward an information-gathering motive. I'm married to Duncan Reed. Which means they have to know I would have electronic copies of everything copied to the cloud. So, I assume they were fishing. Why don't they just kill me?"

Had she said that last part out loud? The room began to spin, the air conditioning system getting louder. She was losing oxygen and needed to stick her head between her knees. Refusing to be a distraction, she remained upright. With her last comment, the others would think she feared death. She didn't. Not her own.

People were already dead because of her. Again. The children she'd left behind when she escaped captivity. Casualties lost when her detective work was too slow. Lucinda.

Eddy cleared his throat. "Early on when I learned the emails had been sent through my machines, I tried to find out who was doing the sending. I couldn't break into what they did to my machine. Just knew the emails kept routing through my desktop unit. I knew I looked guilty as hell. The job had been too good. Too careful. I suspected Parker, but he'd already gotten cozy with the ADA." He tilted his chin toward Miranda. "Respectfully speaking, of course."

Miranda turned several shades of red. Dipping her chin, she lifted a hand and waved him on.

"Since I'd already made some…comments about her. Sorry again. They were all good, by the way. Anything I said was going to come across as me trying to frame Parker over a personal jealous thing. I set up a camera in my office to catch the bastard, but they must have figured out a way to do it remotely. Parker was smart to choose her and to choose my machines. Or else Zheng was smart to lead him in that direction, ya know." He lifted his brows to the captain.

"Apology accepted, Detective," Dave said. "Please continue."

"They're good, that's for sure. Jimmied into my place. Planted this laptop I heard about." He shook his head. "I couldn't break in, but they must have known you'd be able to, Duncan."

Duncan didn't respond. His expression didn't waver either.

"So, I started watching the Reed place. Started following the prick. Parker, I mean. His dates with the ADA."

And just when Nickie thought Miranda's chin couldn't dig any lower into her neck.

Eddy sighed. "He went into Phil the barber's shop."

"What?" Nickie sat up. "When?"

"That's right, Nick. And it was after Phil was murdered. Under the yellow tape and all. Something's in there, man. I broke in and searched every corner. Hell if I can find a damned thing. I had no idea this deal today was going to happen. I followed Parker out of the station. He met up with his black turtleneck pals and the rest is on the books."

"It's good to have you back, Detective," Dave said distractedly. "I'm sorry we ever doubted you."

"It's good to be back, sir. And if the roles were reversed, I would have doubted me, too."

Dave nodded and said, "I know you have more and I have a few questions myself, but right now we need to hear from Dr. Li."

Traci was winded, but she didn't sound traumatized. Not like the ADA and certainly not like Duncan's office manager. She was angry. Her recount of the events was spot on with the evidence.

"I kneeled behind the desk, unarmed, for a half hour, texting whoever I could and listening as they shot innocent people and ransacked the place. At least seventeen perpetrators—"

So, Dr. Li had counted as well.

"— have infiltrated no less than three locales in regards to a trafficking operation that spans the country. I am sorry, Captain, Detectives. I know we don't like it, but I am notifying the feds."

Already done, Nickie thought. Dave knew this, too.

"And I'd like to finish my interview with Detective Savage. With as much professionalism as I can emphasize, this has become personal for me."

Nickie pulled herself up, the determination in Dr. Li's voice giving her a renewed sense of drive. "I'm ready to finish our interview whenever you are, Doctor."

* * *

Nickie insisted they do the interview in her office. It would have been like a stick-it-to-Zheng tribute. She'd told Dr. Li it was Nickie's town and Nickie's station and Nickie's case. Yet here they sat, back in Interrogation 1.

"I see you were fourteen when you were abducted," Dr. Li said as she flipped through Nickie's files, Nickie's personal files.

"Yes." Nickie sighed. There were few things in life she liked less than talking about her childhood.

"By gunpoint in your home?"

"Yes."

"He found you asleep in your bed?"

"Yes." Nickie ignored the dizzy nausea, refusing to stick her head between her legs.

"He coerced you through the window and down the ladder with a gun?"

"Yes."

Traci smiled and tilted her head. "Generally, after the first two yeses, my subjects feel uncomfortable with such unhelpful answers and tend to elaborate."

Nickie smiled in return, leaned back in her chair and folded her hands in her lap.

"You spent eighteen months in captivity?"

"Yes."

"What was the abductor's demeanor during the abduction?"

Ah. An open-ended question. "Indifferent."

"Tell me about the ride away from your home."

That part was fuzzy. "I was taken in a white box truck. Cliché, I know. Duct tape over my mouth and thrown in the back. He was still indifferent. I may as well have been a chicken he carried to the market."

Dr. Li paused and glanced at her before continuing. "Tell me about the first few days. Was your abductor present? What was his demeanor in this atmosphere?"

"You keep saying my abductor. You know who took me. His name is Jun Zheng." Nickie leaned over her files that rested in front of the doc. "See? There's a picture and everything."

"I want to learn his motive. It will help me with who works for him." She leaned back and looked Nickie in the eye. "And over him."

"Over him?" Nickie asked.

"Did he treat you differently from the others?"

The others. Bile rose in her throat. She stood and ran to the wastebasket that sat next to the only door to the room. As she emptied her stomach, Traci said, "If you would have dropped your head lower than your heart when you began to feel lightheaded, that might not have happened."

Nickie wiped her mouth with the back of her hand and stood only to find Traci inches away offering a paper towel. Nickie took it and cleaned herself up.

"He's a bad guy, Traci," she said as she sat back in her spot. "He's *the* bad guy. If you tell me where you are going with this, I could be…more helpful."

"Fair enough, but then I need you to trust me and my expertise."

"You've trusted mine. So, fair enough."

"It will help me if I learn his persona. Examples, details. Not just your assessment, although it is also warranted and worthy."

The last part was patronizing, but Nickie would have done the same and she really wanted to get this over with. "The others meant nothing to him. The girls meant nothing." That was Nickie's assessment. She held up a finger before she continued. "He didn't talk to them or to me at first. Not unless it was time for training or a job."

"Training?"

Nickie stuck her head between her legs and closed her eyes. For that moment, the nightmares behind her lids were a necessary evil. "He needs most of us to submit. Training is his way to make sure we do."

Silence.

Okay. "It involves rape, but never by him. He only does the beatings."

"That helps me, Nickie. Thank you. You've switched to present tense, and that worries me."

She had? "Why does that worry you?"

"I am interviewing a person who just vomited, has her head between her legs and is speaking as if she is there in her past."

Nickie held her hand above the table and moved it in big circles. "I'm fine. Keep going."

"You said he needed, needs, most of you to submit. Why did you say most?"

Her head cleared, and she sat up. The doc's posture was official and methodical. Her eyes were not. Even though her nose was up and her lids partially closed, her eyes were glossy and rimmed with pink.

"Some liked—" Nickie emphasized the past tense ending. "—fighters. I was a fighter. It's why they called me savage. It's why I changed my name. I don't want to forget that time or the girls or my purpose on this planet. I may have been through hell, but that hell made me what I am. That hell has saved others. Kidnapping victims to college rape victims to groups of captive children in trafficking crime rings. I have no regrets."

"Other than the girls you left behind."

The backs of her eyes burned. "What the hell does that have to do with the station mole, Jun Zheng, my father or this investigation? You have about two minutes before I'm outta here."

The doc dipped her chin. "I apologize, Detective. Let's move to your father."

Her shoulders became tired. "What do you want to know?"

"You're a woman in your thirties."

"Early thirties."

"You've had personal experience with victims representing a plethora of types of abuse."

"Barely early thirties really."

"I'd like to hear your thoughts on your father."

"I don't know. I'm not a good judge of parenting." There it was again. Why did she stop taking her birth control pills? She could really use a Diet Coke right about then.

"You'll be a lovely mother."

"Who said I'm going to be a mother?" She answered too quickly. Damn it.

The doc smiled. It wasn't got-cha or condescending. It might have been easier if it was. "You're a giver. You see, some people are takers. They take. Some are traders. They will give, but keep a record expecting something in return. You are a giver. You've been this way since childhood, I suspect. Or at least since the time you were abducted."

What would make her say such a thing? She sat back and slung a boot on her knee. "My father showed no signs of sexual interest in children or that of extramarital affairs, for that matter, if that's what you're getting at."

"Not the facts, Nickie. What do you think? You were there. You know better than anyone. Your view may be clouded with childhood perspectives, but you were there."

"Clouded with childhood perspectives?" She didn't care if her voice was rising. "Regarding my father?"

"Do you think a person could be immune to the effects of their upbringing?"

That made sense. Sort of. She looked to the wall. Gray blocks of concrete. Not helping. She closed her eyes and listened to the thrumming of the relentless rain. "He was indifferent." Shit. That word again. "I was a tomboy. He hated that. He wanted a ballerina, an English horseback-riding cellist. I tried. I talked the talk and walked the walk when it mattered, but then I would sneak out to ride bareback and play my cello freestyle."

"Do you still play?"

"Hmm? The cello. Oh. Yes." Although not lately. "I think it was money. He's always needed a rich life. His import and export business doesn't make enough to fund his lifestyle."

"Yes, I've seen that analysis in your reports."

"More like facts. Two plus two doesn't equal millions."

"Okay."

"He got involved in trafficking, and I stumbled across a room he used for processing." She placed her boots on the floor and rested her forearms on her thighs. "We're doing an informal infiltration first thing in the morning." Her smile was genuine. The doc would know this kind of thing. "That will give the backstabbing prick, Parker, enough time to get all patched up in the hospital."

"I'd like to join you."

"With Parker?"

"No, at your father's home."

Nickie threw up her arms and rolled her eyes. "You and the rest of the world. I don't have a warrant, Dr. Li. I'm going as a daughter who's showing her husband around her childhood home. It might not come across as such to a jury if I've got half of Northridge and a profiler on loan from the city with me."

"Who is the rest of the world?"

"Hmm? Oh. My mother and father-in-law, my foster mom and brother, my brother and sister-in-law, Captain Nolan and now you. I can picture it now. 'Hello, Dad. I'm just here with a few friends, a police captain and professional profiler. We'd like to look around, specifically in the basement.'"

"You're going when he's home?"

"No." She shook her head. "Not my point."

"I'll wait in a nearby car. We'll send you in with a wire."

She was serious. "I thought you were due back home tonight."

"I was."

The doc stuck Nickie's files in her bag. Hey! What if those were her originals? Which they were not.

Standing, Dr. Li paused behind her chair. "I need to reiterate that I'm calling the feds."

Nickie ground her teeth.

"I know that doesn't sit well, but you've had three locations systematically breached by a large organization.

An organization that spans across state lines. This is bigger than Northridge, New York."

Nickie stood as well. "As you've already told me. It's already on the books. Special Agents Hurst and Goodrich. Will you let me do the calling?"

The doc looked at her straight on. "Do I have your word?"

"You do."

CHAPTER 19

Her captain and the profiler rode behind them in a police-issued unmarked. The word awkward didn't quite cover it. Maybe the word gray was more accurate, and Nickie didn't do well with either. She was a cut and dry kind of cop. Gray didn't make it in a court of law.

Duncan drove. It was the only part of this mostly informal operation that made sense. Mostly. Another gray word.

She'd gotten her captain involved. It was not only out of his jurisdiction, but also across state lines. A case that was soon to be solely in the hands of the feds and should be already. The feds that she hadn't notified yet as she told the profiler she would. Nickie deserved a large L painted on her forehead.

She'd come to accept that the case wouldn't be hers much longer, but this part belonged to her and her only. These were her parents. The house was the one she grew up in, well, until the age of fourteen anyway. However, suicidal or stupid she was not. Both her parents and her childhood home were dangerous. She wouldn't step foot inside without backup again. So, she got her captain involved. And Dr. Traci Li. If she listened to all of the people who loved her, she would have Duncan's entire family as well as her foster family with her, too.

"This spot will work well," Duncan said. He pulled over to the side of the country road. Through the clear morning sky, she could see her parents' home in the distance.

Her phone vibrated. As she took it from the inside pocket of her jacket, she winced, ignoring the bandaged wound from the bullet graze. As she did, the back of the audio/visual bug pin brushed the side of her thumb. The pin was a U.S. flag stuck through the lapel of her leather jacket. As if she would ever wear a pin of any kind on the lapel of her leather jacket. Not that anyone in her father's home would know that. She shrugged and checked the text. It was from her captain in the car behind them.

nick?

the surveillance cameras are powerful. we can see both exits from here and still stay clear of them.

k

Duncan parked his SUV behind some bushes as he said, "I understand waiting for your father's vehicle to leave the premises, but as soon as we arrive, the butler will alert him of our presence and he will return."

She checked over her shoulder to make sure Dave hadn't parked too close. "I'm counting on it." Then, she reclined halfway and set one boot on the dash and then the other.

Duncan pulled out a brown paper sack that read Northridge Bakery on the side. "Did you honestly bring donuts?" she asked.

"This is a stakeout. I also brought a thermos with coffee refills."

"No need," she said. "Look." A long, black BMW crawled down the back drive, then turned toward town.

"What if it's your mother only?"

"I say, bring it. We've got no other choice." She let her boots thump to the floor. "Let's give them ten. Don't want them to get back and confront us before we get a good chance to look around."

"Is that enough time?"

"I know where we're going in there." She flipped the tiny switch on the back of the U.S. flag. "Testing visual/audio," she said toward the windshield. Her phone vibrated in her hand.

we can hear you and are looking at the glove box

"Okay," she said to the bug. "We go in ten."

"A watched pot never boils," Nickie said as she sat in his passenger seat. It didn't quite fit their scenario, but it made Duncan smile regardless.

"Shall we recap our plans?" he said, taking her hand. It was more of a test to judge if her palms were sweaty or her hands trembling. They weren't. She wasn't.

"Sure thing." She set the ankle of one of her boots on her knee. "The butler answers. We go to the basement room. I repeat that I know where we're going. That comment was meant for Mr. and Miss Nosy in the ugly unmarked behind us. We make sure to rotate and talk as we walk so said Mr. and Miss Nosy get a visual."

"If and when your mother and/or father return, we confront them with what we know." Duncan considered this point. "Why is this again?"

"Fishing. Perps make mistakes when caught off guard." She laced the fingers of their joined hands together. "After seventeen years, I suddenly go right to the room? They don't know I saw your hypnotist. This will be a big caught-off-guard moment."

She referred to her father as a perpetrator. The label was accurate, and yet her smile and sarcastic demeanor disconcerted him. He'd learned both served as a mask.

She gripped his fingers tighter. He assumed she didn't realize this. Lifting their joined hands, he kissed the ring on her third finger.

He heard the long inhale followed by a heavy sigh. "It's okay, Duncan." She must have sensed his aversion to her manner. "Other than the night of my abduction, I don't have nightmares from this place."

Other than the night of her abduction? He had no words for this.

"I mean, I was in a…" She closed her eyes. "Never mind. Let's do this."

"Signal me if and when you need to abort. I am here for you."

"You mean like a secret signal? I could pat my shoulder twice, then the top of my head once."

He steered away from the shelter of the bushes, his tires crushing the gravel. "That would work at Wrigley Field, but maybe inside of this particular location you could simply tell me it's getting late."

She smiled. It was the first sincere expression he'd seen on her beautiful face all day. "You are," she said, then added, "here for me."

Pulling out onto the highway, he took the turn toward the Monticello mansion. Duncan stopped the SUV so the security cameras could pick up Nickie's face, which meant they had approximately ten minutes from that time until whoever was in that car—Edward or Ivanna or both— could make it back to the house. There was no use dwelling on either since the wrought iron fence was opening.

The blue sky led the way as he trolled through the dark, towering evergreens. Forcing his breathing to slow, he maneuvered around the circle drive and parked in front of the marble steps leading to the front door no one was expected to use.

Nickie squeezed her pant leg that hid her spare gun, then reached up and released the snap over her holster. "We're going in," she said, dipping her head toward the audio/visual bug on her lapel.

Leaving the SUV doors unlocked, he dropped the keys into the pocket of his suit jacket. Nickie wore her MO. Black boots with thicker four-inch heels, black slacks and a fuchsia three-quarter-length sleeved blouse that was unbuttoned to just above her cleavage. She held herself with the most confidence using this line of wardrobe. It was likely his suit served the same purpose.

Her parents, however, would disapprove. Will disapprove, he thought, as he checked his watch. Eight minutes. Ignoring the bell and the enormous metal knocker centered on the massive door, Nickie rapped the wood with her knuckles.

She rotated to the left, then the right. Yes, allowing Captain Nolan and Dr. Li a view of the perimeter.

A familiar face cracked the door open. "Clarence!" Nickie jeered. "There you are! You remember my husband, Duncan."

Clarence didn't offer a greeting. "Just as last time, ma'am, the mister and missus aren't here." He smiled at the floor in front of her, then added, "Yet."

"Nice touch, pal. I'm counting on it." Her warm hand wrapped around Duncan's and pulled him over the falcon made of stones toward a hallway on the left.

She hadn't been exaggerating about knowing the way to the room. She marched without pause to the third door down the hallway on the left. Cameras hung from each corner and one from the center of the hallway ceiling. Hand in Duncan's, she opened the door. A descending stairwell stood much like the rest of the home. Stone steps with thick, dark wood followed the winding path and served as the railing. And cameras. They were everywhere. "I feel as if I should wave," he said.

Knowingly, she laughed. "I get that." Then, she did. She lifted her arm and waved to a corner unit. "Hi, Mom. Dad. Cheese!"

They wound down the spiraling stones. At the bottom was another hallway that spread to the left and the right. Still holding his hand, she squeezed tighter and led him left again. Her steps became shorter and her shoulders dipped inward, her chin dropping an inch. It was slight, but he didn't miss any of it.

She stopped at the only door with a rubber guard along the bottom. Soundproof barrier. This was it. His empty stomach churned.

"Duncan, um, ow."

Oh. "I apologize." He released his tight grip on her fingers.

With her hand free, she reached for the antique brass knob. He grabbed her wrist. "Should we use gloves?" he asked. His detective always required gloves.

"Gloves say investigation. I'm a daughter in this scenario, Duncan. Are you gonna be all right?"

Closing his eyes, he dipped his chin. "Yes, of course."

She gripped the knob and twisted but it didn't move. "Your turn," she said, backing out of the way.

The instruments in question waited in his pocket. Reaching in, he dug around for the one he needed. He pulled out a metal file, inserted it into the lock, closed his eyes and felt for the mechanism. "This is wrong," he said and tried a smaller file. Trial and error, his years in the military paid off as the lovely sound of a click opened the door.

He turned to see his Nickie leaning against the wall, arms crossed, on the opposite side of the hallway. "I didn't want to pressure you. We are in a sort of a time crunch though."

As he turned the knob, he heard it. Suction released from the thick rubber soundproof barrier. He imagined the walls, as well, were lined with additional materials. It made the hair stand at the back of his neck.

Inside was a storage room. High quality wooden shelving covered each wall. Wooden boxes with centered labels were stacked in each compartment. Painting supplies, hoses, drywall materials, PVC piping. He started for the end of the room toward the next door.

"No," she said. "This is it."

He turned and took another look. "This?"

She nodded as she rotated in a complete circle. Stepping up to a second shelf, she anchored a boot, then grabbed the top of the structure with one arm. Using her body weight, she extended her loose arm and leg until the entire unit tipped. Boxes slid. She jumped out of the way just before the entire structure crashed to the floor. Exposed was a scuffed wall with a line of several dusty outlets.

"Just as I remembered," she said.

"Nickie, what does this mean?"

She tilted the audio/visual bug, then rotated it along the exposed area.

"There was a line of desks here. I remember at least a half dozen old school computers. Over—" She meandered to the other side of the room and pointed to another set of shelving. "—here. This hypnotism memory feels like what you must see with your eidetic memory. I see it all. This is where mattresses lined the wall." This time, she pounced. She grabbed hold of the shelves and yanked, catapulting out of the way as a much louder crash echoed through the area.

Beneath the unit were stains in various colors of brown. Blood and urine. He'd prepared his heart for this, and yet...

"Soundproof walls," she said as she jumped, yanked and catapulted one shelf after another, each with more force than the last.

This was needed. He understood and stepped out of the way. First, she hollered in triumph as the next set of shelves came crashing to the concrete floor. By the last, tears streamed over her artificially smiling cheeks.

The sound of thrumming feet made both of them stop. Duncan heard five sets. Clarence ran in out of breath and was followed by four men dressed in black pants with matching mock turtlenecks. "I'm calling the police," he said.

"Go for it, dude," Nickie said as she pulled down the last of the units.

The man closest to her simultaneously grabbed her shoulder and wrenched her around to face him as he slapped her cheek with the back of his hand. Two stepped toward Duncan, but the red rage that filled the corners of his soul raced his autopilot into overdrive. He swung a left hook at one, connecting a solid punch to the temple, then used momentum to return with an uppercut to the second. This man flew backward to the ground, and Duncan charged for Nickie. She stood, fists clenched high and ready to fight, but Duncan was already in the air. The rest of the room became an empty field of black. He wrapped his arms around the man who had struck his wife and fell to the ground with him. The man sailed an elbow into Duncan's jaw, but it was of no consequence. Duncan felt nothing but waves of pounding red as he threw one punch after another at the man's head until the man lay still.

Duncan drew his gun as he jumped to his feet and swung it around to face the others that threatened Nickie. A round of clicks erupted as each person faced one another and pointed their guns.

"No need, Clarence." The voice had become familiar. Too familiar. Etched in his eidetic memory forever. It was followed by the steps of designer shoes as Edward Monticello entered the room.

No one even flinched his aim.

Edward tsk tsk'd as he scanned the area and Nickie's destruction. "Drop your weapons, gentlemen." The men left standing obeyed, then stood at ease. He glanced toward the one bloodied and unconscious who lay behind Duncan, then moved his gaze to the two who sported large, red circles on their faces.

"Hi, Dad." As if all had been resolved, Nickie shoved her gun in her holster and turned back to the exposed walls. Reaching in the pocket of her leather jacket, she took out her mini-camera and clicked off pictures.

"Nicole," Ivanna roared as she stepped out from behind Edward.

Edward's thugs took a step forward, but Edward held up a hand.

Ignoring her mother, Nickie finished with the photos, then turned and faced her father. "I know," she said and tilted her head. "And now you know I know. What are you going to do about it? Shoot me like you did Leslie Jacobsen? Phil the barber? My partner?"

Duncan circled his fingers around her upper arms. Her skin was moist, her muscles tight and shaking.

"Or just offer to let your boss come and take me by gunpoint?" These last words she said through her teeth.

He stepped closer to her. Close enough that Duncan placed his shoulder between Edward and his wife.

Edward ignored him. "You've completely lost any piece of sanity you might have retained from this…this lifestyle you've adopted."

"Duncan," Nickie said. "Looks like the blast-from-the-past tour is over with."

It was like the parting of the sea. The six of them stepped away, leaving a narrow path for him and Nickie to use. Slowly, they walked, Nickie with her hand resting on the butt of her Smith and Wesson. Duncan wasn't willing to holster his Beretta.

In the absolute silence, tension buzzed electrically from body to body. It was deafening especially to Duncan's eidetic hearing. Eyes darted between the mess in the room, Nickie's hand on her gun and the pocket where she'd stowed the camera.

He and Nickie rotated as they passed, then stepped backward the rest of the way out the door and down the hallway. No one followed them.

Two black SUVs idled in the circle drive. A single driver sat in each. Duncan opened Nickie's door, placed his hand on the back of her shoulder as she lowered into the passenger seat, then swung the door closed. He got in and started the engine. Nickie waved as they passed their observers.

The vehicles rolled behind them, following all the way to the wrought iron gate.

"Take a left," Nickie said to Duncan, then spoke louder. "Dave, we have a tail. We're breaking left."

Captain Nolan and the profiler were to the right. With the obvious tail he and Nickie had, Duncan understood why she would want him to turn away from Dave and Dr. Li. About a quarter of a mile out, the black SUVs pulled to the shoulder and stopped but didn't turn around.

"I'm taking her to the intersection of 1040 E and highway 16," he said loud enough for Dave and the profiler to hear. Nickie didn't argue the point. She'd gotten her camera out and was studying the photos she'd taken inside the room her father used to house captive children. It was difficult to conceptualize the scenario, so his mind fought the idea.

In his rearview mirror, he spotted Captain Nolan's unmarked. "Nickie." He placed a hand on her thigh. "Dave is behind us."

Her chin rotated toward the side mirror. "He has a tail." Then, she spoke up. "Dave," she said loud enough for the bug to pick it up. "You have a tail." She took out her phone and dialed. As her cell rang, she said, "It's one of the black SUVs. Duncan, he has to see it. What the hell?"

"Do I pull over?" he asked more to himself than to Nickie. Squinting in his side mirror, he noted a discrepancy. "Uh oh, Nickie. Those aren't your father's men."

"That's not singular, Duncan. The men driving Edward's SUVs were singular."

Duncan rolled his wheels onto the shoulder, then turned his eyes to Nickie. Simultaneously, they said, "Hurst and Goodrich."

CHAPTER 20

Nickie clenched her hands in her lap, brainstorming possible scenarios and excuses. She was going to call? It was the next thing on her list? This was simply a preliminary scan of the place? Lame, lame and lame.

Dave pulled behind Duncan. The SUV behind Dave. Dave and Dr. Li stayed in their car. Both black doors of the SUV swung open.

The two weren't dressed in black slacks with matching mock turtlenecks. They wore suits with semi-fancy shoes and ties. Hurst's large frame towered over the vehicle. Hot summer sweat glistened around his dark face and sparkled in his buzz cut. Goodrich took his time, adjusted his sunglasses in the driver's side view mirror and straightened his shirt collar.

She squeezed her eyes shut. It wasn't like she didn't know this was going to happen, just not yet, not now. Mostly, she was scum. Hurst had stuck his neck out for her more than once, and this day was nothing less than sneaking behind his back.

Duncan's voice usually soothed her. Not this time. "Am I to assume you did not tell Special Agent Hurst you discovered the mole was Officer Parker?"

It was a rhetorical question, and she didn't have the energy to answer rhetorical questions.

Hurst went to Duncan's side, Goodrich to hers. Reluctantly, she pressed the button that rolled down her window.

"Detective Savage," Goodrich said as he stood tall. "We'll be escorting you back to Northridge where we will take Officer Parker and Jun Zheng into federal custody."

They already knew about Officer Parker. Of course, they did.

"At that time, we expect," Hurst said loudly from the other side of Duncan's car, "for you to turn over the camera you used while searching your parents' home. We've already confiscated the recording equipment from the audio/visual bug from Captain Nolan."

Her camera? The personal camera she bought to record evidence in her preferred old-school fashion? Not in this lifetime. Sucking in a quick breath, she opened her mouth. "Ow." That was not what she'd planned on saying, but Duncan had squeezed his fingers around her knee hard enough to hurt damned bad.

Goodrich shook his head as he walked away.

"Hey, what was that for?" she asked while rubbing the spot on her knee.

"Special Agent Hurst made it so we have the five-hour drive home to copy the photos." He plucked the camera from its resting spot between her legs. "This mature device does have email capability, doesn't it?"

"Be nice to my mature device. It makes me happy. And, thank you. You're right. He did do that, didn't he?" She sighed and considered before adding, "Do we trust that one?"

"I think we have no choice."

"Or else he's buying his time and working us."

"A cautious trust, then."

"I love you. You're amazing."

* * *

Duncan's arms ached to grab Special Agent Goodrich by the shoulders and yank him out of Captain Nolan's chair. The captain, the profiler, Nickie and Duncan took up the chairs, which left Special Agent Hurst without a chair. No one offered to retrieve one for him.

Agent Goodrich twisted side-to-side on the captain's high-back roller chair like a child. "Detective Savage," he said from the safety of Dave's desk. "Jun Zheng is wanted on charges in connection with—"

"Obstruction of justice, kidnapping, child trafficking and murder," Nickie interrupted expressionless. "If you're going to take him, get on with it."

"You also have the officer in custody who was involved with Mr. Zheng."

Nickie rolled her eyes. "You make it sound like they're lovers," she said.

Duncan thought it was perfect. Officer Goodrich did not appear to agree.

"We'll be transferring him to a secure federal facility as well."

"Good luck with that. He's in the hospital with a bullet in the shoulder, a broken nose and a dog bite to the thigh."

Goodrich sighed. "We'll need proof of vaccinations from the dog."

It was their dog, and Goodrich knew this. Nickie glanced at him through half-opened eyelids.

"And the complete notes from the profiler."

Oh no. Duncan looked to Nickie. That interview was personal.

She jumped to her feet. "When hell freezes over," she said through her teeth.

Goodrich sniffed and checked the fronts and backs of his fingers. "And any other files on this case or any other involving Jun Zheng or trafficking within a sixty-mile radius of this area."

She set a single hip on the edge of the desk and craned her head to the side. "I have things you need," she murmured.

Goodrich's eyes dipped to the hip Nickie stuck out. "Like the pictures on your personal camera we will soon have in our possession? The ones you took in the basement of Edward Monticello's home? They were obtained without a warrant and will never be permissible in a court of law."

"Have you done your research?" Duncan asked. "The detective's record regarding what is and is not admissible in court is rock solid."

Goodrich pointed his finger at Duncan. "You're only here because of your involvement, Mr. Reed. One more word and you will be escorted from the premises."

Dave stood this time. "Whoa, whoa, whoa. This is my house."

Nickie stood in the circle of angry eyeballs and held up her arms. "You're right."

Duncan could hardly believe his ears.

"The visit I made to my parents' home was too obvious. There isn't a jury alive that would believe my objective in my parents' home was to simply share it with my husband."

It was never her plan to achieve reasoning for doing so, only to do so. Duncan wondered what her motive was for the direction she was taking. Since Agent Goodrich was mostly distracted with her protruding hip, Duncan backed away.

"I went directly to a single room and destroyed it." She rotated and placed both palms flat on Dave's desk, then leaned toward Agent Goodrich. "I have locations that match the evidence found in the Monticello basement. I've…" She closed her eyes, inhaling deeply and smiling slightly. "You know I've been on the inside. I have locations, addresses. And I know how to get Officer Parker to talk. Partner with me and I'll promise full disclosure."

Silence lingered in the air like fog. Agent Goodrich's eyes wandered between the cleavage that was surely evident, to one side of her, then the other.

"Special Agent." Hurst spoke louder than necessary for the size of the room. "I'd like to speak with you privately for a moment."

Goodrich nodded and the two of them exited the room. The cloud of despair lifted, if only temporarily. "Nickie," Dave pleaded. "You won't win with this."

She crossed her arms and leaned back on Dave's desk. "You're probably right, but I don't see another option."

"Nickie." This time it was the profiler, and Duncan had a feeling he knew what she was about to say.

Nodding again, Nickie said, "Don't. I get it."

"I'm not a therapist. There is no confidentiality clause in this situation. I could lose my jo—"

"I said I get it."

Agents Goodrich and Hurst came back in the room, this time with Goodrich standing in front of Nickie. It was a common tactic used by small-minded men who attempted to physically intimidate women. He crossed his arms and said, "Tell us how you plan to partner with us, Detective."

The muscles in her jaw flexed and released. It killed him to watch her roll over and succumb. "I'll give you the first location. Duncan and I go with you."

"A civilian?" Agent Goodrich huffed a half laugh.

"A civilian advisor who's gotten through more of this case than both of you put together."

Goodrich clenched his fists at his sides. "And Parker?"

She started pacing. "Let me at him. Piece of cake."

"I'm going to tell you my dilemma, Detective," he said and rocked back on the heels of his shoes. "This case keeps getting bigger and bigger. Agent Hurst thinks you're valuable. I'm not feeling it."

Nickie turned her neck until it cracked, then did the same to the other side. She pulled out the to-be-confiscated camera and thumbed through the pictures. Stopping at one, she turned the screen to Agent Goodrich. "See this? These are scratches on the walls in the basement of the Monticello home."

Goodrich tilted his head one way, then the other as if he doubted her.

"They're in the outline of a square. A square low to the ground. They are made from a cage. It's where Zheng puts girls when they're either being punished for noncompliance or else locked up because they haven't been brainwashed enough to be trusted not to run."

Goodrich curled his nose and took a literal step back.

Nickie responded and closed the sudden distance between them by stepping uncomfortably close to him. "Do you see the yellowed and dark brown stains, here?"

"I know what that is, Detective."

"There are identical marks in Henderson."

Goodrich held up both hands. "Nice try, Detective, but we already know about that location."

She glanced to Duncan. He willed her not to say it, and shook his head.

"I have a map."

"A map?"

"Yes, a map." She rotated on the balls of her feet and walked a circle around all of them. "And I'm not turning it over." She said the last part using her fingers to make quotation marks in the air.

"That could be considered obstruction of justice."

She shrugged and continued strolling, lifting her gaze to Agent Goodrich. "I got nothing to lose."

"You have your job to lose."

She shrugged again. "Like I said."

CHAPTER 21

The heels of Nickie's boots stuck to the floor under the standing table in front of her. She gripped her glass of water carefully so as not to get a splinter from the table. This was The Pint. The place cops were supposed to go to decompress, vent and, in this case, celebrate. It was not a place to bring the family.

"I don't feel much like celebrating," her partner said from across the table.

"You're the man of the hour," she said. "You deserve this. You were set up. Shot. You pegged Parker, watched my place. And you're not a backstabbing mole. You deserve a week…no a month of celebratory drinks."

Eddy shook his head. "Don't say all that, Nick. We lost the case to the fucking feds. There is no worse shit to be had."

"A toast to the detective's assessment," Duncan said and lifted his frosted glass.

She had been moving her straw around, trying not to suck up any seeds from the single slice of lemon in her water. Deciding to be a team player, she lifted her glass and clinked it against the others.

"I missed the toast?" The ADA plopped her purse on the only empty space and sighed. "I'm sorry, Eddy, but this sucks. They took everything. Confiscated every file and paper." Lifting Eddy's half-empty bottle, she held it toward the light, then downed the rest of it.

"Hey," Eddy said and took the bottle from her. "This is my party. Get your own."

"Chivalry is truly dead," she said and made off toward the bar.

Nickie went back to her straw. As she sipped, she scanned the place. The whole atmosphere was bittersweet. Death, homecoming, loss, closure…even if the closure sucked.

Warm air blew the hair that covered Nickie's right ear. She turned just enough to get a whiff of beer mixed with mint gum. It was the ADA. "Traci Li wants to speak with you," Miranda whispered. "She's waiting in a booth in the back."

Nickie blinked and looked down toward Miranda's pumps.

"And if you tell either of these two gossip girls," Miranda spoke up so everyone could hear and waved a finger between Duncan and Eddy, "I'll never confide in you again."

"Never," Nickie answered. "Girls rule."

"Another round, ladies and gentlemen?" Duncan interrupted. "I'm buying."

"If my boots aren't permanently stuck to this floor, I'm gonna pee," Nickie said and pushed away from the table.

As a rule, she didn't sit in the booths at The Pint. She was sure the original upholstery covered the seats, and who knew what had been done on them over the years. Nickie spotted Dr. Li's shiny black bob. She wore the same navy blue pantsuit she'd been in since early that morning.

Sinking into the seat across from her, Nickie tried not to think about the upholstery. "What a day, huh?" Nickie said.

Dr. Li took a deep breath. Her gaze traveled all over the table before landing on Nickie's. "I needed to apologize."

"I don't know what you need to be sorry for, but did you need to do it in secret like this?"

"No, but I needed to apologize first. I am the one who notified the FBI of your raid."

Raid? Nickie and Duncan searching her parents' home hardly counted as a raid. "I figured."

The doc had the nerve to look honestly surprised. "You did?"

"Detective and all that."

"Right. I still believe this is too big for a local police department." She held her hand up like she thought Nickie was going to argue. She wasn't. "But asking for my files, the personal ones, is going too far."

"What are you saying, Doc? You gonna cover for me?"

She nodded, her short, black bob moving with her.

"Okay. I didn't see that one coming."

"I haven't written out my report yet. My notes are written in a special shorthand I created. The notes won't make sense to them. I'm going to give you the real report verbally and..." She sucked in a breath like the words were stuck. "I'm going to give an abbreviated report to Special Agents Goodrich and Hurst."

"I gotta be honest with you, Doc. Not that I don't want to be grateful and everything, but I've got all sorts of red flags popping up in my head."

Nodding, Dr. Li took another deep breath. "My professional assessment of you is that you are trustworthy. Over all else, you do the right thing...even if it means sacrifice. So, I'm going to do the right thing. And that means trusting you."

"It could be a sacrifice."

Dr. Li shook her head this time. "I don't think so. I won't break the law. Scratch that. I am breaking a direct order and that could be considered the law, but no." The doc shook her head again. "It's all quite gray. I don't have a lot of time. Detective, I do not believe Jun Zheng is the top of this Fu Haizi, as you like to call it."

It was Nickie's turn to sigh. She prided herself in her ability to keep an open mind. This was not happening at the moment.

"He is too hands-on, Nickie. Too physically acute. He doesn't fit the profile, if you will pardon my unintended pun. He is a worker bee, as we like to think of them. Zheng is important. Don't get me wrong. I am both relieved and hate that the special agents have him in their custody."

"You're trying to tell me my father runs this, aren't you?" She hoped the doc didn't have the same aversion to rhetorical questions that Nickie did. "He's not a pedophile. We've already been over this. He never laid a hand on me. No physical intimidation whatsoever. He got plenty mad at me as a kid and never once used physical force. You're telling me he's the king pin of Fu Haizi?" Oops. She was not whispering in their covert booth any longer.

Holding up a finger, the doc leaned in farther. "Nickie."

Lowering her raised hand, Dr. Li placed it on top of Nickie's. Her knee-jerk reaction was to pull it back, but she didn't. A painful instinct scratched at the back of her mind. It told her she didn't want to hear whatever the doc was about to say.

Dr. Li's fingers were small and soft. They wrapped around Nickie's as Dr. Li whispered, "I believe the top, the king pin, as you say, of your Fu Haizi is Ivanna Monticello."

Nickie's chin dropped to her neck. Her eyes moved from one side of her seat to the other before she craned her neck far to the right and squeezed her eyes shut. Heat built in her gut, spreading outward to the rest of her body. "My mother," she croaked. She'd spent her teenage and adult life convincing herself the bizarre relationship with her parents didn't matter, that she had a foster mom who loved her and that it was more than most people got. She had the job. She had Duncan. It was more than she needed because, "I don't need anything or anyone."

As she realized she'd said that last part out loud, she squeezed Dr. Li's fingers and pulled her hand away. "You're crazy, doc."

"You see," Dr. Li said softly as if Nickie hadn't just dissed her. "You provided a detailed scan of your childhood home from several angles and rooms. Nickie, I was able to watch and analyze the video feed of your parents as well. It is your mother who makes the decisions."

Nickie let her back rest against the seat. "Doctor, I regard your position with the utmost esteem. The plethora of cases you've solved is commendable. However, I need to respectfully decline your analysis and get back to my group."

"You've lost your purposely unrefined demeanor, Detective. Right now, I expect your heart is racing and your skin is cold with sweat. You know I'm right, and I'm here for you."

Nickie glanced down at the sheen forming on her exposed forearms, but no words came to her. From her peripheral vision, she noted a pair of black gym shoes and tight dirty jeans marching toward their table. Nickie glanced at the waitress and shook her head. The expression on the woman's aged face fell. With wide eyes, she looked between Dr. Li and Nickie, then nodded and backed away.

Dr. Li paused, then pulled out a handful of photographs from the pocket of her navy blue suit. "I thought you might be reluctant to accept my assessments. These are some still shots I took of the feed you so skillfully provided."

She panned them out over the table. They were in chronological order spanning from the time her father had entered the storage room in his basement. Dr. Li didn't need to explain. Nickie saw it now.

"This is when they walked in. Ivanna stood behind Edward."

As she always does, Nickie thought.

"He's her cover. Nickie, I don't think he knows. Not everything, anyway. Look at this one."

The expression on her mother's face was shock, anger. Nickie remembered the moment. It was when Edward told his men to drop their weapons. The next photo was when her mother yelled at her, using the birth name Nickie had purposely eradicated. Her father held up a hand. Behind him was her mother glaring darts into the back of his head. But it was the picture of her mother when Nickie stepped to her father and challenged him with the deaths of Phil the barber and his employee, Leslie Jacobsen. She'd stepped back and dropped her chin in that shot.

Dr. Li's expression said she knew what Nickie was thinking. "What happens now?" Traci asked.

"I can't believe I'm going to say this, and if you ever tell anyone I said this, I'd have to kill you in your sleep, but I think you should tell Hurst and Goodrich."

Traci nodded. "There are three things I refuse to give up. The first is anything that has to do with your relationship with Detective Lynx. The second, personal details about your history with your parents. And third, that you might be pregnant."

"What would make you say that?"

"About number one, two or three?"

"You know which number."

"Fair enough. You've changed since a few years ago when I last worked for your department. You're softer, warmer. And frankly, nicer. You are a beer-drinking cop in a bar celebrating the return of your partner with lemon juice on your breath."

"Maybe I'm a on a diet, a few years older, married and in love?"

"Maybe."

CHAPTER 22

———◆———

By the time Nickie returned, several additional men in blue had joined the celebration. Duncan couldn't imagine what the Assistant District Attorney could have possibly told Nickie that caused her to retire to the back of The Pint for so long, but he stepped aside and made room for her nonetheless.

Wrapping his hand around Nickie's waist, he moved her glass of lemon water to the spot he'd created for her, turned to the ADA and whispered, "It seems as if you have an admirer."

The medical examiner approached from the bar, two martinis in hand. The appearance of the ADA and the ME was certainly compatible, she in her tailored skirt and blouse and he in his pressed plaid shirt. "Extra dry," he said to her and winked.

"Thank you, Benjamin," she said. "I'm sorry for what you are dealing with in your lab this week."

Benjamin dipped his lips close to Miranda's ear, but not close enough for privacy. "Never mind that." He raised his glass, then said out loud, "Celebrate!"

Duncan tugged Nickie closer and she leaned into him, lifted her glass and clinked with the growing crowd. "There are six precincts here," he said to her. The slight lavender aroma that seemed to follow his wife everywhere filled his senses.

She smiled, but it didn't reach her eyes. "I'm happy for Eddy."

"As am I." He couldn't quite read the expression on her face. It seemed to say that she didn't believe him. "He's been there for you. If he crosses the line, he will suffer the consequences. He and I have a mutual understanding about this."

The man of honor came from the bar balancing a serving tray over his head. "Fireball shots!" Two waitresses followed him, each with their own serving tray. He held up the tray as loud police officers emptied it one by one as well as the ones from the waitresses who accompanied him.

"A real drink for real men," he said as he handed one to the ADA. "How about you, Nick?"

Duncan placed his hand between Nickie and the shot. "We will be boarding a plane right about the time you arrive home this evening."

Eddy shrugged and raised his glass. "Tonight we honor the ones we've lost. They may not have been men in blue, but they were family." He placed the glass to his lips and threw back the fire.

Miranda stuck her nose to her glass and inhaled. This was never a good idea. She clutched her eyes shut and held it at an arm's length. Duncan took it from her hand and threw it back before anyone noticed.

His detective pressed her lips to his cheek and kissed him before moving her mouth to his ear. "I need to talk to you," she said.

He nodded. "I know."

Nickie sensed it. The weeded drive was too weedy, the deserted house too deserted.

"Do you feel that?" Duncan asked her.

"Nothingness. Glad to hear you say that. Now, aren't you glad I didn't tell Hurst and Goodrich about our little trip?"

"You promised two FBI special agents that you would share the locations discovered on my brother's map." The sexiest, evil grin spread over his face. "So, yes. I am extremely pleased with your decision to make this trip without them."

"Goodrich made it clear they already knew about this location and had no need to revisit."

"You added the last part."

"There are disadvantages to being married to a man with an eidetic memory."

A small crease formed at the spot between his eyes. "This town is clearly one of the locations on the map Andy created. It can't be a coincidence."

He was preaching to the choir.

As the tires of the rental crunched over the gravel in the drive, he mumbled, "Without question, Officer Parker chose Henderson as one of the locations to route his dozens of dummy trails."

A blast of cold air blew on her face from the vents. "And since this is a house previously used to contain trafficked children of Fu Haizi," she added in equal frustration. "Something's going on." Impatience scratched the back of her neck as she opened the car door before it came to a complete stop.

Duncan rolled to a stop as her boot hit the drive. Stepping out, she stood tall and faced the property. A single-story unit, it would seem small to a passerby. However, she'd been inside and knew it had a basement, something uncommon in Nevada. The basement would be the reason Jun Zheng chose the location.

This time here was different for more reasons than the vacant appearance. She wasn't sweating, even though it was at least twenty degrees hotter than last time. No lightheadedness. Was it because she was with Duncan instead of crooked feds who were using her for her knowledge of child trafficking captivity?

"Well, we flew all the way out here," she said and stepped through the blistering heat.

Weeds slapped her pant legs as she waded through them on the way to the back door. It wasn't latched. She flipped open the snap on her gun holster. As she pulled open the screen, the inside door inched away, creaking louder than a haunted rocking chair in an ancient attic.

Duncan placed one arm in front of her and the other at a ninety-degree angle. He made a fist, then pointed to his ear. Military signals. Attention. Listen. She married a veteran. And she heard the noise, too. Muffled scratching and rustling. Sliding her gun from her holster, she took it off safety.

Holding it near her cheek, she stepped around the door and into the small kitchen. A million particles of dust stirred in the beams of sunlight, disturbed by the light breeze. Each cabinet door was ajar, some more than others, exposing empty shelves that were covered in filth. Duncan pointed to her chest, then to the far left side of the area that led to a small living room. Then, he pointed to himself and to the right side, toward the basement door.

"Like hell," she mouthed and crept toward the noise. No footsteps or voices, but movement came from the basement. Keeping vigilant of both her surroundings and silencing her footsteps, she crept along the floor on her toes, careful to dart her gaze between the living room opening and the basement door.

The door leading down was open, a line of locks and deadbolts hanging free. Gun extended, she placed one foot, then the other on each step. Pressing against the stairwell wall, she kept a lookout both up and down.

As she descended, low groans and mumbles became apparent. Back against the last piece of wall before the stairway ended, she craned her neck around. Dirty mattresses littered the area, but they weren't lined along a single side of the room and there were no cages, desks or computers.

She sighed and slid her Smith and Wesson back in its holster. "I'm not here to bust anyone," she announced and turned the corner. The group of them scattered like ants.

Squatters. The basement windows were barely enough for a child to squeeze through, but one-by-one they made it regardless. A mixture of body odor, marijuana and urine blew around the room as the window swung on its hinges again and again. Six of them. Well, five if you didn't count the one not bolting at the sight of her gun and badge.

"They're not hurting anyone," she said to Duncan. "I don't have it in me to rattle their cages."

"We flew all the way out here," he said exasperated. "Are you sure about this?"

"I have some other ideas," she said, considering the one who remained.

He eyed her as he sat on one of the mattresses and leaned against the concrete wall.

"You're not running," she said to him.

His eyes said he was alert. The track marks on his arms were few. His hair and clothing were filthy but not faded or torn. He shrugged. "I got nothin' to lose."

Oh yes, you do, she thought and asked, "How long have you been here?"

Shrugging again, he said, "I don't know. A few months, I guess."

"More like a few days," she retorted. "I'm Nickie Savage. This is Duncan."

"Savage," he mocked. "How did you get a name like that?"

"If you only knew," she said.

"And if you know all about how long I've been here, why did you ask?" He crossed his arms and didn't attempt to leave or even move.

Nickie sat on the backs of her heels in front of the mattress. "What's your name?"

"Jane Doe."

Smart-ass. She liked this kid. "Nice to meet you, Jane. How old are you?" She guessed fifteen or sixteen. And she guessed he wasn't going to tell her that.

"Old enough. I thought you didn't have it in you to rattle my cage?"

"Oh, that's not rattling," Duncan said as he lowered next to her. "The detective's rattling is not pleasant. I suggest you answer her questions, or you could find yourself crying for whatever mother you have out there."

"Let me put it this way," she edited. "How long have they been here?" she asked, pointing to the last pair of feet as they exited the window. Answers lie with this boy, not with the stoned group running down the streets of Henderson, Nevada, at that moment.

"Heard 'em talk about being here during the World Series."

World Series poker in Vegas. "That was almost a year ago," she said. "Why are you here?"

"I told you. I got nothin' to lose."

"Do you have parents who care that you're gone?" She understood the first part of her question didn't necessarily mean the last.

"Would I be here if I did?"

"Maybe. I can hook you up with a roof over your head that includes food and decent people."

"I ran away from that place," he said through his teeth.

"Are we talking group home or foster care?"

"Both."

"There are good ones. Both kinds."

"Do I need to jump out the window now?"

Standing, she let her lungs expand. "I can hook you up with one of the good ones."

She saw the consideration in his eyes before he lowered his lids to half open.

"Will you take my card?"

Rolling his eyes, he held out his hand.

She grabbed the pen she kept stuck in her belt and wrote her personal cell on the back of the card.

He took it and tucked it into the back pocket of his jeans before crossing his arms again.

She turned to face him straight on and squinted. "You're not the only one who lived with the bad ones. I ran away from plenty of those places when I was your age."

He didn't move his head, but his expression turned into a mixture of curious and hopeful. They stood like this for a long moment. Assessing her, she supposed. "If you take me in, I'll get away again. I know how to work the system."

Reaching out, she wrapped her fingers around his forearm. Non-threatening physical touch. "I can help you. That's my personal number. You can call anytime, day or night."

She stood and nudged Duncan with her elbow, then nodded toward the stairs.

CHAPTER 23

"Where are we headed?" Duncan asked Nickie as he shifted his rental into reverse.

"Downtown. I'd like to look around."

He maneuvered out of the drive as he said, "I am trying to be cognizant of the fact that both the foster care system and living-on-the-run are your expertise."

"Is this about the good cop/bad cop tag team we did with the squatter? I've never seen that side of you. I almost jumped out the window."

"We left a minor in an abandoned house."

"He already escaped the system. He'll do it again."

"You could have told the authorities what the boy said about working the system and getting away. You could have gotten him into a secure facility."

"The system failed him. It's likely he was molested or abused. There are good foster families out there. There are also bad ones. Very bad ones. He wants help, but he needs to come forward on his own."

"You could lose your badge."

"Are you making a citizen's arrest?" She asked, smiling in his peripheral vision. "I also happen to be sleeping with an artist with an eidetic memory who might just draw me a detailed sketch of the boy that I can use to run a search."

He lifted a corner of his mouth. "Bribing me with sex. That's a dirty tactic."

"We're married. I can do that." She ran a hand over his thigh and…his eyes nearly popped from his head.

"Ah, yes. One custom drawing and a search through COTIS thereof in exchange for whipped cream and the sheer cami I bought you for Valentine's Day."

"Turn here," she said.

"The empty house concerns me, Nickie."

"I don't know about that. The cluster of hits thing on Andy's map wasn't specific to the address, right?"

"Point taken."

"Two minds create a third, more powerful mind."

He loved this woman.

"Here's good," she said. "I'm actually looking for someone in particular."

As he stepped out onto the asphalt, the line of sweat down his back was almost instantaneous. Bare, red mountains towered beyond the end of the long road that led out of town. She actually waited and allowed him to open the car door for her.

"Yes," she said. "Just as I remember."

A mom-and-pop grocery store squeezed between a barbershop and a massage parlor. What more does one need? He held open the door for her and stepped into the pitiful air conditioning.

Tight rows of short shelves lined the dimly lit room, a row of refrigeration units towering along the back wall. A young girl, no more than thirteen, stood behind the cash register eyeing him.

"Hello," Nickie said to her. "Is your mother here?"

"I run the place." Her smile was tired, worn and sincere. "What do you need?"

"I need your mom, actually. Do you know when you expect her back?"

The question apparently lifted the child's concern. She looked at Duncan, then to Nickie, then toward a backroom.

A woman with too many lines for her young face entered the room with purpose in her step. "I'm the owner. What do you—?" Eyes stopping at Nickie, her feet came to an abrupt halt.

The woman and his Nickie stared at each other for longer than comfortable, the girl looking from one to the other.

"You can come to the back," she said to Nickie. "I have coffee in the break room."

Duncan was not at all comfortable with this.

"I'd like that," Nickie said and left him standing there.

"How long have you worked here?" he asked the child while watching the opening to the backroom as well as listening for any signs of distress.

"Since I was old enough to walk." Her voice had turned defiant. "I've been store manager since I was ten."

As if she could be much older than that now. Store manager? He wondered if her mother would agree to the title. "Impressive," he said and pretended he was browsing through the Red Bull and candy bar display near the single register. "That's quite a resume. Do you like it?"

She picked up a clipboard and started flipping through pages. "It pays the bills," she said like a grown-up.

He liked this girl already and fought back a grin. "Well, then I think I'll take this." He placed a handful of single-serving peanuts and three packs of gum on the counter. "And this as well," he said and added a few cans of the Red Bull and Snickers. "Snickers satisfies," he added and made her laugh.

"Mama lets me up here all by myself now." Her voice relaxed into that of a young teen. "I don't make any mistakes."

"None? My, my. I imagine your mother is very proud of you."

Her smile was lovely and completely contagious. "That will be $18.04."

He handed her a fifty-dollar bill, then looked around the counter. "Do you have a tip jar?" he asked.

She looked at him as if he were an alien. He supposed for

R.T. Wolfe

all intents and purposes, he was. "No, and we don't take fifties."

"Well, since that's all I have, maybe you would just keep the change for me. I am intensely in need of this Red Bull." His Nickie might possibly be willing to eat the peanuts and maybe a piece of gum, but he'd never seen her eat candy and the Red Bull would be considered worse than the Diet Coke she'd been depriving herself of.

"You want to give me an extra $30.96? What are you, a billionaire?"

"Not nearly, and it's $31.96." He lowered his brows. "Why aren't you in school?"

Her face turned red as Nickie came from the backroom followed by the mother. Reaching for his hand, Nickie squeezed his fingertips.

"Thank you," the woman mouthed to her.

Duncan took the generic plastic bag of items from the young girl, then placed his hand on Nickie's damp lower back. They walked to his car in silence. He opened the door, and she thanked him. This caused him significant suspicion.

"Ya know," she said as he slid into the driver's side of the rental. "Sometimes this job is okay."

"Tell me."

"I questioned the mom last year when I was here."

He knew there was more and reached over to twine his fingers with hers. "Shall we make any other stops before we leave?"

"No. I got all I need." She gripped his hand as he listened to the sound of her cleansing breath. "She had the daughter in hiding last year when I interviewed her. Afraid Jun Zheng and his men might take her. I guess there was a lot of that going on around here back then. Thinks I saved the day and all that."

"You did. And more so."

"I can't consider Fu Haizi moving the location of a group of girls from here to another spot as saving the day. The bad just changed where it was. Good on her, though. Her kid's cute."

"She needs to be in school."

"Survival. At least they have each other."

"Which brings us back to why we are here."

"Right. If the house is deserted and the town has been safe for almost a year now, Fu Haizi moved, moved. And not just neighborhoods."

"Then, why the cluster of hits on Andy's map?"

"Exactly what I was wondering."

"Two minds," he repeated.

"There was a cluster in Baltimore, too," she said staring at the magnificent horizon.

"Your parents' home."

"Which is also deserted."

"How does this moment find you?" Duncan asked as Nickie pecked away on her laptop. She sat at the wet bar in their ridiculously large master bedroom.

"It looks like the boy was telling the truth," she said, scrolling through his records. His cheek brushed against hers as he investigated the laptop that glowed on the granite top. The warmth of his face was like blood pressure medicine.

"Ah. The Henderson runaway. His name is Jane Doe?"

"Very funny." The scent of Duncan's barely there cologne was a pleasant distraction. "He's been in four foster homes in as many months. Ran away from each. Two of the homes have complaints filed that were deemed unsubstantiated."

"And his parents?"

She shook her head. "Mom is MIA. Dad is doing time." Not the same as her childhood, but close enough to sting. "I found a legit halfway house and a few good foster homes. None are close, but I don't get the impression he'll mind getting away."

"How will you find him?"

"He'll call." She had to believe that.

He rubbed his cheek against hers.

"You shaved," she said and bathed in his proximity. Her head turned to him without her telling it to. Her lips rested on his. This was what home was. He moved his lips to her forehead and brushed the spot near her hair. Opening her eyes, she smiled. "You're naked," she said and pulled away for a better look. "When did you get naked?" A smile spread across her face, and she wrapped her arms around the back of his neck.

He didn't answer. But he did press his lips to hers, their mouths moving together as one.

"I am not," she said between kisses, "naked."

Pulling her shirt from her slacks, he slid it over her head. "We can fix that." Seamlessly, he unbuttoned and unzipped as his lips became as needy as the parts of him in her hand.

"I never have enough of you," he groaned as the muscles in her legs threatened to fail her.

She knew what he meant, yes. Her hands traveled around and down, across and over. His quick intake of breath made her smile. "This is different," she said. "Everything is different." He kissed her harder, his hands running over her flesh and cupping her backside.

"And now you are naked with me." He lifted, and she wrapped her legs around him, heat finding heat. He carried her like this toward the bed. "Tell me what is different," he murmured, out of breath.

Could she tell him? The thought of it made her feel more naked than the lack of clothes. He sat her on the side of the bed, and his lips moved from her mouth across her jaw and to the place just behind her ear. Her heart raced, her skin warmed, but it didn't change the different part. It only made it worse.

He moved close enough that the heat from his body covered her in waves. She clasped her feet behind him. Her head fell back, and she looked at the stars through the skylight window in the ceiling. His tongue moved over her neck and down the void in the center of her collarbone. His fingers linked with each of hers, and he pulled their joined hands outward.

"You're magnificent." He trailed his lips lower and circled one side of her, causing a low purr to escape her throat. The circling became tighter until his teeth centered and pulled.

"Oh," she moaned and lifted her head. "This is different because we are making a human," she confessed. "It's natural and primal. Like purpose has been added to the physical and emotional." His torturous tongue traveled farther. He blew on the wet line he'd left. "I had a hard time with control when it was just the physical and emotional."

"So, leave the blasted control," he said as he reached her core.

His mouth knew her well. She went over in seconds, fast and hard, the sounds coming from her throat uninhibited. Some kind of foreign instinct took over, and she reached around, grabbing hold of his fine backside with one hand and the part of him her body demanded in the other.

She expected him to say no, not yet.

Duncan didn't know what came over him. He never allowed this so soon, but her declaration of making a baby took over everything else. They moved together in sync, as husband and wife. He grasped one of her shoulders and wrapped the other hand around her back, anything he could do to get closer. Closer to the warmth, to the meaning behind this moment.

Her body melted around him, a layer of sweat forming between them making their movements that much more potent. He felt her tighten and clamped his eyes closed. The cliff. He fell off the edge into euphoria and trust. "My Nickie. My wife," he said. Her nails dug into his backside as she went over again. Sexy alto whimpers escaped her perfect lips as she released her blessed control.

"Again, again. Duncan, don't stop."

Her words were more than any man could be expected to withstand. His face burrowed into the crook at the side of her neck, and he inhaled the intoxicating lavender that followed her everywhere. He went over into another place, somewhere meant for just the two of them. His voice betrayed him as well, groaning to the moon and beyond.

They held, pressed, then held further, his face burying

into her hair. Together, they stayed there, wrapped around each other so tightly it was difficult to tell which limb belonged to whom. "I fear my arms and legs are locked here."

Her cheeks expanded against his shoulder.

"We may need to stay like this forever."

CHAPTER 24

———— ◆ ————

They didn't let Duncan come with her this time. It pissed her off, but she had to hedge her bets, and right now, they were letting her in. Hurst drove. Goodrich rode in the passenger seat. They put her in the back. She didn't even care about that. It was the girls. She was here for the children, not Hurst or Goodrich. Oh, how she hated agency testosterone, red tape and bureaucracy. The victims never seemed to come first anymore. Had they ever?

No one spoke as they traveled the familiar road to her parents' home. The black suits and ties in the front seats made her want to loosen the collar of her navy blue blouse. She tried to distract herself with busy work on her tablet. Focus was a challenge since they'd brought what seemed like a fleet of FBI black SUVs. It was embarrassing overkill. The convoy could be mistaken for the mob. That was what she would think if she spotted it. They were car number two.

What would they even find? She already had everything she needed from her parents' basement. The room. She shivered. This was going to be a wash. She could feel it. Yet, she tagged along. For the children.

The wrought iron gate was open and they turned in without pause. Her eyes traveled to the house. The evergreens lining the drive waved at them in the wind as they passed between them.

Straightening in her seat, she waited as Hurst followed behind FBI car number one. She ran her hand over the top of her head, then took hold of the back of her neck.

As if orchestrated, they parked at staggered locations around the perimeter of the manor. She got out before the SUV came to a complete stop. "Detective Savage—" Goodrich began.

There was nothing he could say that she wanted to hear, but she paused and listened like a good girl.

"We'll do the talking."

He did not just say that. It made her left eye twitch. "The woman should be quiet? Bite me, sir." So much for the good girl. She slammed the door behind her. Goodrich followed up the stairs, then stepped in front of her before she reached the immense front door. It stood, slightly open, light pouring through the crack it made.

Reaching inside a compartment on her belt, she pulled out two plastic gloves.

Goodrich pushed the door open and peered around. "We'll need to wear gloves, Detective."

She held out the ones she'd taken from her belt and shook them in front of his face before slipping them on and ducking beneath his arm.

"Federal Bureau of Investigation Special Agents Goodrich and Hurst," he yelled. "Is anyone home?"

That was a mouthful. No one came. Just the two of them stood in the foyer. Hurst was nowhere to be found.

"We have a warrant. Hello," he said.

She walked back to the front door, then rapped on it with the backs of her knuckles. Six special agents came in as she did, nearly running her over. "Is there a fire?" she asked. Something wasn't right, and not just with the emptiness of the house.

"Please show us the way, Detective," Hurst said as he came through the front door. Oh, now they need her.

"Down that hall," she said, pointing to the left. "Third door on the left is a stairway. Follow the basement hall to the end. It's on the right. Can't miss it."

He lowered his brows but followed as the men thumped their shiny black soft-soled shoes toward the way she'd explained. She decided to look around up here. "Clarence," she called. No answer.

Walking like a tourist in a museum, she strolled toward the kitchen. It might have been the middle of summer, but the stone floors and walls seemed to keep the place damp and cool year round.

She found her father there, a drink in his hand. Checking her watch, she shrugged. From what she remembered, her father never had his first drink before evening. The translucent brown substance in his crystal glass seemed a bit strong for noon, but at least it wasn't morning. Technically.

Digging her boots harder into the ceramic floor, she let them announce her entrance as she walked in. His eyes turned to her. Bloodshot and swollen, with dark rings beneath each. She had to take back her earlier assumption. Apparently, this wasn't the first drink of the day.

He stood leaning, or that could have been lying, on the counter separating the nook area from the rest of the room. His clothes were wrinkled, his shirt half-untucked. She could see part of his large stomach as it hung over his pants.

"You," he said.

"Pops."

Squinting his eyes, he turned back to gazing out the walls of windows lining the back.

"Where is she?" Nickie asked.

"Gone."

Gone? "Wow." She lifted her brows. "Didn't see that one coming. Not with you here anyway."

"What did you expect?" he slurred. "This is your fault." As if his words made sense, he turned to her. "This is your fault." This time he said it as if he'd had an epiphany.

"Umm." She didn't want to guide him anywhere other than where he was going. Except, she didn't know where he was going with this.

"Always making trouble. Ever since you were a child."

She swayed her head back and forth. "There is that. Where's Clarence?"

"Gone with your mother, I believe."

"Where is gone, exactly?"

He shrugged. "Hell if I know. She took everything."

Nickie lowered her brows and looked around. Large table in kitchen nook. Eight white-painted metal chairs around the table. Rack full of wine glasses. Plants in planters, brass artwork hanging on the walls.

"Ouch," she conceded and rested her forearms on the granite counter next to him. He reeked of sweat and alcohol. "It's not over."

"That's what she kept saying. What's not over?"

"There are men here that have a warrant for your arrest."

"Let them," he said and threw back the rest of his liquor.

She stared at him. Yes, something wasn't right. Hurst walked in with a SWAT team wannabe she recognized as one of the men who had passed her on the way to the basement.

Hurst looked around. The wannabe spoke. "Edward Monticello, we have a warrant for your arrest. You have the right—"

"The room was clean," Hurst whispered in her ear. "It smells like fresh paint."

"Duh," Nickie said.

"Why is he still here?" Hurst asked. "You get anything?"

"Don't know and nope." She was being rude. He didn't deserve it. "He's significantly intoxicated. Maybe after he sleeps a while. A meal might help."

"This must be hard for you. I'm sorry," he said.

"Thank you, but no need. That was a long time ago."

"Today is not a long time ago. Today is now."

* * *

Renting a car for the trip from the airport to the prison would have been wasteful. Nickie convinced Duncan to take a taxi. He hadn't argued with her about it. This concerned her.

Heat pounded down on the puddles, making waves in the air like a desert oasis. "I slept the whole way. I wish you would have woken me."

"It wasn't the whole way."

"I stayed awake through half a foot rub. Yum, by the way." She sneaked her hand beneath his as it rested on his leg. "I could have come alone. I'm keeping you from prep for your show."

"I count one wish to have been awoken and one that I would have come alone. You are my wife. The show isn't for a few days yet, and the preparations are complete. You needed the sleep. You can't keep up this pace much longer."

"So, you've told me."

"What are your objectives for visiting William Tanner, if I may ask?"

Right. They were supposed to go over all of that on the plane ride from Rochester to Terre Haute.

"I want to question him about my mother's alleged involvement in Fu Haizi."

"Alleged?"

Ugh. Right again. "Not alleged. I'd like to at least judge his reaction to the mention of her name. If she's some kingpin…." The idea almost made her laugh out loud.

"It's been some time since you last interrogated *Captain* Tanner." He said captain as if it were a dirty word.

"Former captain. Former pedophile, crooked cop captain. I'm also going to throw out the name of the john I killed."

The watchtowers came into view over the flat Midwestern skyline.

Duncan watched out the window as well as he continued. "Captain Tanner—"

"Former," she amended once more.

"Former, disgraced and rotting-in-prison Captain Tanner has not been as helpful in your latest visits."

"I thought about that. Same ole, same ole. He's been comfy too long. I have to put him back with the regular population for a few days. Since prisoner types can't stomach pedophiles, he'll get the shit beat out of him. Then, I come back and offer to return him to his private cell in exchange for information that's actually useful."

"It is quite a dance the two of you do."

Her phone rang before she could respond. "Savage."

"Detective, it's me."

Caller ID said Slippery Jimbo, and it sounded like Slippery Jimbo. But Jimbo never called her Detective. It was Detective Dude or Nick, when she would, then, need to rough him up.

"You there? It's me, Jimbo."

"I'm here. Why are you calling me so early? Aren't you supposed to still be sleeping?"

"See, that's the thing. I wasn't sure if I was stone—I mean drun—I mean too sleepy. Or if it was real."

He was talking too fast and his words were slurred. "Are you still stoned, Jimbo?"

"No. Slept it off. But last night, man. I saw things."

"I'm on a job, Jimbo. Call me when you have something for me that's not a hallucination."

"I don't hallucinate moving trucks, Detective Dude. When I hallucinate, it's more of big titties and—"

"Stop. Tell me about the truck, or I'm hanging up."

"So, I stepped behind the alley of Get Lucky's to take a piss."

She didn't believe him already. "They don't have johns in Get Lucky's anymore?"

"Soooo, I might have been having a smoke."

"People smoke inside Get Lucky's, Jimbo. They even smoke shit that ain't tobacco. I'm hanging up now."

"You a smart one, Detective Dude. My woman dumped me, man. She took me for an arm and a hand. I was out back getting a blow—"

"Hanging up now, Jimbo."

"A truck. A big truck pulled up to Phil the barber's."

"Phil the barber's? The deserted Phil the barber's shop with ragged yellow tape around the front and back?"

"Yep the very one. Somebody was shacking up in the place."

Squatting she could believe, but squatters don't use moving trucks.

"They had a bunch of somebodies shacking up in Phil the barber's old shop. You told me to keep an eye on the place, and I am, Detective Dude. I am one a-ma-zing official police informant."

Because he noticed a truck while getting blown in an alley? "Did anyone see you? Or the…woman you were with?"

"Oh, that. No. The woman. See. I was standing and she was sort of down, ya know."

Yeah. She knew.

"They had to have at least fuckin' ten, maybe twenty people in there, dude."

"Explain."

"They moved out at least a half dozen mattresses. And some cages."

Her lips parted. Heat poked her shoulders, up her neck and filled her head. Phil the barber's? How? When? Why?

"Detective Dude?"

"Where are you now, Jimbo? Are you sure you weren't made?"

"Piece of ice cream, Detective Dude. I know how to be unseen."

"I want you to go right to the station, Jimbo. I'm telling the captain you're coming."

"Aw, fuck me, man. I hate that place. It gives me hives."

"You can wait in the break room. I'll have coffee and donuts sent in."

"You're not even there, are you?"

"No, but I will be." She looked to Duncan. "I'll be there soon," she lied. "I'm calling the captain. He'll be expecting you."

"I don't know…"

"Jimbo. These are the same men who hurt you. Go now. Please."

"Fuck. All right. No need to get your panties in a bunch."

She hung up and stared at the back of the taxi driver's seat. Fu Haizi had girls in Northridge? "How? When? How long?"

"We will find out," Duncan said. She'd said the last part out loud?

Weights pressed down on her shoulders. The sweating started. Her mouth watered. A gentle hand pressed between her shoulder blades, pushing her head between her knees.

"Shall I instruct the driver to turn back for the hanger?"

"No," she said to the dirty floor mat. "I need to talk to Tanner." Duncan would understand. "I have even more questions now."

The car slowed to a stop. She heard a sliding metal door open, then the cab driver said, "Dropping off some visitors."

She raised her head, but not too fast. She didn't want to explain that she wasn't hiding but trying not to puke. "I'm Detective Nickie Savage," she said to the security guard checking her out. "From Northridge, New York PD. I'm here to interview an inmate." She used the manual crank to roll down her window and stuck her badge through the opening.

He took it and stepped inside the small booth. Damp heat poured through the open window. It was no bother. She was already sweating. Fu Haizi. Set up in her hometown. Now, she was pissed. How long had they been there? There had to be a friggin hidden room in Phil the barber's place.

"Detective?" The security guard waited with her badge held out like she was dense.

She took it from him and nodded.

"The visitor's lot is to the left," the guard said to the driver as he pulled away rolling up his window.

"Zheng will pay." It was Duncan's scary voice. He must have interpreted her conversation with Jimbo.

Guards stood holding rifles in tall towers around the perimeter, each with an additional man sitting in a chair keeping watch. Although she couldn't see the university from here, it still amazed her that it was in such close proximity to a maximum-security federal pen.

"Here will do," Duncan said as they neared the visitor's entrance. She didn't wait for him and instead got out and walked at a fast clip to the entrance. Her mind demanded time to sort through Jimbo's intel. It would have to wait.

Northridge was not one of the clusters of IP address hits on Andy's ingenious map. The place had been used by Fu Haizi for years; it appeared as a meeting place, not a holding place for a dozen captive trafficked children.

No. She was here. She needed to rough up Tanner. That would help. He was going to tell her about the last john who she was sold to and about her mother in Fu Haizi. And if he didn't, he was losing the cozy solitary room she'd bargained for him and would be thrown back into the pedophile-hating regular housing he deserved to be in.

Entering the first waiting room, Duncan chose a small table and opened his tablet. Nickie paced. Her body was rested from her nap on the flight over and her mind a buzzing hive of possibilities.

She barely made it two laps in the waiting room, ignoring the dirty looks from the other visitors as she passed them. The checkpoint guard must have alerted the inside guys of her coming. Ushered through the second set of doors, Nickie eyed the wonky expression on her escort's face. As they entered the room where she would empty her pockets and be searched, Nickie released the buckle on her holster.

The checkpoint guard held up a single finger. "Detective Savage?" she asked like she was surprised to see Nickie.

Nickie froze her hand on the buckle and said slowly, "Yes."

"You're here to see William Tanner."

"Yes," she said even slower. "Is that a problem?"

"I'm afraid it is, Detective. He was found hanged in his cell this morning."

CHAPTER 25

His Nickie had spent the entire flight home in one of the few seats on Duncan's plane that actually looked like an airplane seat. Former Northridge Police Department Captain William Tanner was dead. Hanged in his cell in an alleged pitiful attempt at suicide. Pitiful due to the abrasions she was told were around his wrists.

Who had access to his private cell? Duncan assumed that was what Nickie had been sorting through her mind on the flight home. He had worked on his laptop, giving her the space she needed to process the information that had been thrust upon her already overworked and under-rested head.

Touchdown didn't provide a reaction, so he said, "Are we headed to the station?"

"Duncan, I have a bad feeling about this. All of it. My parents' home was wiped clean, Phil the barber's spot emptied. Tanner hanged." Her cell rang. She checked the Caller ID, then answered. "Savage."

As she tilted the phone away from her ear, Duncan was able to make out the voice, just not the words. Nevaeh Thornton.

"I'm so proud of you, honey." Nickie's voice dripped with pride. "Of course I'll be there. Text me the time." She hung up and swiped, then typed on her screen.

"She is a testament to your work," he said.

"Thanks." Nickie shrugged. "She's doing a training session at her college. Hits home."

The place where Nevaeh herself had been drugged and raped.

"Her trainer from Child Rescue will be there. It's a training session for trainers, so that ups the ante for her, too."

"And you will be there for her."

"It's the least I can do."

The plane came to rest in the spot he owned in the hanger. "Nevaeh is not a trader."

She stood and looked at him now. "Is this the taker/trader/giver thing?"

He took her face in his hands and smiled. She blinked three times. "Yes. You make it sound as if you owe her. Like you, Nevaeh is a giver and does not require restitution for what she has done."

"I love you. I don't know where I would be without you."

He brushed the side of her soft cheek with his thumb. "You would be right where you are. Saving college girls from rape and children from Fu Haizi. And you would be supporting all of them. Just as you are now."

Her grin was slight but sincere. It disappeared as quickly as it came. "I started my period this morning."

He blinked, then blinked again before resting his lips on hers. "In time, my wife."

"No," she said.

Fear seeped into his spine. He pulled his face back and looked into each of her eyes. Her damned phone rang again.

"No, let's not head to the station just yet," she said as she checked her Caller ID. "I want to stop at Phil the barber's first."

The relief nearly buckled his knees.

"Savage," she said into her cell and stepped away from him.

He would have to get a grip on his emotions regarding

the possibility of a child. All in time, he repeated in his mind. Or not. He couldn't allow himself to rely on the chance.

"Jane Doe. You called. What can I do for you?"

She stepped toward the pilot as he opened the hatch for her. Duncan wrung his hands together and lifted his chin, filling his lungs with fresh upstate New York air.

"Yes. I found an excellent home for boys…for young men and a few recommendations for good foster homes. I could put in a word for you at either. My connections would get you in."

Her voice wasn't nearly as warm, but her smile was deep and sincere. Yes. Duncan's future was not contingent on a family. He loved this woman. She was the focus. He would not allow hopes for anything else to cloud what he held in his hands and his life.

Nickie had Duncan pull into the alley. She hadn't called Jimbo to let him know what time she would get to the station. She hadn't even told him she was out of state when he called that morning.

She mostly wondered why she hadn't heard from Eddy as to why Slippery Jimbo was spending the day in their break room.

The alley behind T & As, Get Lucky's and Phil the barber's. It was the armpit of Northridge. The strip mall owner got away with the slime and mounding garbage, because none of the shop owners cared one way or another.

Without her asking him to, Duncan knew to park a few doors down from Phil's. A collection of cigarette butts littered the area around the deserted barbershop. She glanced up and down the street. The bars would have noonish patrons in them by now, but no one that might run the risk of slipping into the alley. She put on a single glove and gave the back door to Phil's a shake. Locked. She looked to Duncan. Knee jerk.

He responded by slipping a hand inside his suit jacket and pulling out a ring with a dozen small instruments. He worked the lock for longer than she expected, but it finally opened nonetheless.

Muddy footprints of all sizes littered the ground in a path from the back door to the barbershop break room that had doubled as a Fu Haizi meeting room and storage for large boxes of guns.

The prints led to and disappeared under a pantry door. She took hold of the knob and the door opened with little effort. Inside was a stack of shelves holding two combs and a box of kitchen garbage bags.

Duncan shut the door and ran his finger around the perimeter. Stopping at a spot along a side, he pressed and she heard a click. The entire pantry including the frame popped toward them a few inches. He looked to her and lifted a single brow before slipping his fingers behind the frame and pulling the door toward them the rest of the way.

Concrete stairs led to a basement. The stench of urine and metallic odor of blood wafted up and covered her in filth. She expected this, yet it stabbed at her heart anyway. A blanket of grief wrapped around her torso, threatening to pull her into the abyss. "This damned place has been here all along. Right under my freaking nose." Using years of trained resilience and the ability to stuff just about anything, she took the first step. Then, another and another.

The place was like a cave. The walls had been carved out. Steel beams spaced close together held up vertical ones that carried the weight of the ceiling. A string hung from one of the beams. She pulled it and a single bulb lit the room. A row of rectangle stains the size of mattresses lined one side of the area. A few the size of dog cages lined the other. Two sets of four holes in the floor where two tables must have been placed. Duncan squatted inside the form of one of the rectangles left from the vacated mattress. "These stains are fresh," he said, glancing down at the brown residue from what she was sure was a patch of blood.

She took out the old-school mini camera she'd replaced for the one Hurst and Goodrich had confiscated and started taking pictures. "This is my house," she said much like her captain had done in reference to his turf. "The more I consider it, the more my mother fits it all. Who dismisses their only daughter without the blink of an eye? I was never in trouble with the law or boys. Never much more trouble than a regular young teen. I was a front. The perfect front. My family a hiding place. When I became a risk, she turned me into collateral."

Her cell rang before she could finish the statement. No need. He knew what she was going to say. Turned her into profit. The thought churned his stomach and filled his head.

It was her partner's ringtone. She swiped and placed her phone between her shoulder and ear, taking pictures as she listened. The voice on the other end was not that of Eddy Lynx, Duncan could hear from where he stood.

"Slow down," she said. "You're with Eddy? Okay, okay. Are you safe? Where? I'm on my way."

CHAPTER 26

Nickie thrummed the heel of her boot against the floor of Duncan's SUV. Patience was not her specialty.

"Top floor." She pointed up as he turned into the hospital parking garage.

"The ADA is with Detective Lynx," he repeated in a low voice as calm as if they were having scones with his aunt on Sunday morning. His driving was a direct contrast, the tires of his SUV squealing around each corner.

"Not with him, with him. Lynx wasn't satisfied with just the one fed assigned to guard Parker's hospital room, the backstabbing mole. Miranda wasn't satisfied with Lynx there seeing as he still isn't healed himself." She rubbed her hands over her face. "I know, I know. It makes my brain hurt, too."

"The suspect is male?"

"Yep," she said as Duncan made the last corner to the top of the garage.

"How much time is Lynx giving you before he calls Captain Nolan?"

"However much time I want." She turned to read the expression on his expressionless face, then lowered her brows at him. "That was a reverse psychology question."

He nodded as he tore into the closest spot. "Something like that, you could say," he answered.

She would have double-parked in front of the doors, but it was close enough.

She slid from the car and shut the door running. "The feds probably already have backup on the way. Hospitalized or not, I'm going to use the breach as an excuse to step in and interrogate the bastard."

"That's my detective."

She would never admit how much she liked it when he called her that.

"I'm giving Parker about ten minutes to give me something I can use before I—" she said as she turned her back to the door, pushing it open with her butt as she used her fingers to make quotation marks in the air. "—lose my job for not notifying the feds that the hospital room has been compromised." She took the stairs two at a time, letting the burn in her thighs distract her from that possibility.

The top floor was quiet, worse than hospital quiet. A few nurses stood huddled at the nurse's station. Three doctors stood against the far wall, whispering as she and Duncan strolled out-of-breath toward the corner room that held Parker, Eddy and the ADA. The chair outside the traitor's room that should be holding the federal guard sat empty. It made her check her surroundings thoroughly for possible Fu Haizi.

The sound of a whimpering female came from inside the room. She could hear it before she had a chance to breach the doorway. Pulling her gun from her holster, she held it down at her side. Without causing a top floor hospital panic, she peered around the doorway. The whimpering turned out to be more of a hyperventilating, but the thing she checked for first was the end of the hospital bed and feet she assumed were Parker's under the white sheets.

As soon as she breached the entrance, she held out her gun and let it lead her deeper inside. It was then that she spotted an extra set of feet, lying on the hospital floor next to the bed. Feet wearing shiny black shoes and pressed black pants.

It was the guard. The federal agent. Although in disbelief, she made her feet continue. The ADA stood on one side of Parker, gasping with tears falling down her cheeks. Eddy Lynx stood on the other side of the bed, like a guard over the body.

Eddy shot a federal agent? "You shot a federal agent?"

"He, he, he," Miranda stuttered. "He tried to kill me. Shoot me."

"So, I shot him." Eddy shrugged.

"I'm not telling you anything," Parker said loudly around the bandages that covered his broken nose.

Shoulders shaking, Miranda continued. "He waited until Eddy left to get us all coffee. He even placed an order for three creams and two sugars. Then, he came in and started putting this into Parker's IV." She held up a tissue between her thumb and forefinger she used to lift a syringe. "I asked him what he was doing and, and, and he said he was supposed to. That he knew what he was doing. As if I could be that dense. I told him to stop or I was…" She clamped her free hand over her mouth. "He put the syringe in the port anyway. We struggled. I don't know when he pulled out his gun, but he aimed it at me. I heard a click, but it was—" She started sucking air in short gasps.

"It was me," Eddy finished for her. "I put a bullet in his back."

"He saved my life." The syringe shook in her hand.

Duncan gingerly took it from her and held the end to his nose.

"It's okay now," Nickie said. "We're here."

"You hear me," Parker yelled like she wasn't standing two feet from him. "I'm not telling you shit."

Nickie craned her chin back. "I didn't ask, you backstabbing mole."

Duncan wore gloves and held the syringe to the light. "Odorless. Likely potassium chloride." Where did he get gloves?

"But, since I'm not looking to inject you with anything lethal," Nickie added to Parker. "I'm the best friend you've got, asshole. You know how this works. I can't help save your worthless life unless you give me something good."

Duncan held up a finger. Nickie glanced at his eyes and read what he was trying to say. He knew something. His eyes traveled from Eddy to Miranda to the door.

"Listen, Lynx," Nickie said. "I need you to get Miranda to the station before she passes out." Miranda didn't even argue with her.

Eddy's expression was priceless. "Me?" Yep. Chivalry was dead. She tried to give him a do-it-for-me look.

He threw his head back. "Aww, hell. Come on, woman," he said and stepped over the dead body like he was stepping over a sleeping dog. He may have spoken like an ass, but he slid an arm around her shoulder and guided her out with his other hand on her elbow.

Duncan put a finger to his lips. Parker's eyes grew wide, and he shook his head back and forth violently. Stepping to the television set that hung from the ceiling, Duncan took hold of a knob at a bottom corner and yanked. Not a knob. He examined both sides as he made his way to the bathroom.

A quick plop was followed by a flush. He called from the bathroom. "It has GPS as well as audio. I'm going to flush another time or two. Let them try and trace that."

But she wasn't paying attention to what he was saying. She was more concerned with Special Agent Goodrich, who stepped into the room with his gun drawn. Everything crawled to slow motion.

Goodrich didn't look down at his dead fellow agent. He didn't even look at Parker, who was trembling so hard the bed shook. He stared down the barrel of his Glock that was aimed between Nickie's eyes.

She refused to hold up her hands or even close her lids. She wondered if Duncan would get out of this alive. What he would feel when he saw her lying with a bullet in her head. How they never got to have the family they'd finally decided on.

The single pop was loud, firecracker loud. Her eyes grew wide. So did Goodrich's. He looked down at his chest, but nothing was there. The hole would be in his back. Just like the stiff on the floor. He grabbed his shirt anyway and fell forward like a tall tree chopped down in the woods.

Standing behind Goodrich was his partner. Special Agent Hurst stood with his elbows still locked, eyes staring down the barrel of his Glock. His chest expanded and contracted like he'd just run a mile. Maybe he had.

"What. The. Fuck. Have you done?" It was Parker who asked, breaking the silence.

"I followed him here," Hurst said, gun still extended. "I had my suspicions. Is everyone okay?"

Nickie answered, "Everyone except two federal special agents."

Duncan spun out of the bathroom and dodged around Hurst. "I heard a gunsho—" His eyes traveled to Goodrich who lay facedown on the floor.

Hurst spoke before Duncan had a chance to. "We need to get moving, Detective."

"How deep does this rabbit hole go?" she asked him.

Hurst shook his head and eyed Parker as he lay in his bed. "I'm not sure, but I bet I know someone who does."

With the bug flushed, Parker didn't seem as anxious to loudly declare his code of silence. "Can you walk?" Nickie asked him.

He didn't answer, but didn't argue either.

"This was all about killing you, dude. We're all you've got."

Parker nodded. "All right. Get this shit off me," he said and lifted the arm with the IV and blood pressure cuff.

Nickie's cell rang. Duncan and Special Agent Hurst whispered as she answered while pulling stuff from Parker's arm.

"Ow," Parker yelled.

"Nick. We've got trouble." It was Eddy.

Blood dripped down Parker's arm. Duncan's hand came around her with some gauze.

"Eddy," she said into the phone as she stepped out of Duncan's way.

"There was a car down here. I think it was Fu Haizi people. They took off when I approached."

"They've got friends and family," she said to Duncan and Hurst.

Parker said, "Fuck," and swung his legs over the side of the bed.

"Do you have clothes?" she asked.

"Do I have what?" came from the phone.

"Not you, Eddy. I'm hanging up. Stay by your phone."

Parker scanned the room.

"No time," she said. "Move." She gave him a push in the middle of his back toward the door.

"I've got him, Nickie." Duncan grabbed the back of Parker's arm. "You ride with Special Agent Hurst. We're meeting up with Abigail."

His horse? Oh. The farm. "Good idea." No one would find them there.

She followed behind with Hurst at her side. He shut the door, then shook it to make sure it latched. "Let's discuss the rabbit hole, Detective."

She inhaled, then blew out a breath. So, Hurst was the real deal. And she'd been sneaking around behind his back. "You," she barked at the charge nurse, ignoring the huddle of doctors. "He's coming with us."

The nurse opened her mouth like she was going to argue.

"Anyone opens that door and they face a felony indictment," she yelled and swept a pointed finger over all of them. "Backup is on the way."

She could see Duncan's cheek expanding into a smile as he escorted a barefoot Parker into the elevator. Never before had she been more thankful for hospital robes that covered the backs of gowns.

Hurst stepped in last. They turned around and the doors shut in front of them.

"Am I going to get some clothes?"

"Shut up," they said in unison.

CHAPTER 27

Nickie rode in Hurst's SUV as they followed Duncan's Jaguar.

She dialed her captain's number.

He answered on the first ring. "Nick? Are you okay? Eddy called. We have four squads on their way."

"Be careful. We aren't sure how many Fu Haizi are out there."

"In the words of my favorite detective, bring it."

He was making her smile at a time like this. "Thanks, Captain. I'll keep you updated."

"Where are you headed?"

"I can't tell you. I'll keep you updated," she repeated.

"I'm holding you to it."

She hung up and dialed Eddy. "Where are you?" She hoped she wouldn't get the same answer she'd just given Dave.

"On my way to the Reed Farm. Mr. Whipped called," he said, referring to Duncan. "I dropped off Miranda and picked up Slippery Scumbag Jimbo before the captain kicked his ass and was charged with police brutality."

"He made me ride in the back!" Nickie heard Jimbo yell before the distinct sound of Eddy shutting the bulletproof glass window leading to the back of the car.

Eddy said, "Why did you send him to the station anyway?"

"Long story. I owe you. I…guess we'll see you there."

"Rabbit hole," Hurst reminded her as soon as she disconnected. This rapid-fire shit from all angles was going to have to stop before her head exploded.

"I'm not entirely sure, either. Did the profiler tell you about her theory regarding my mother?"

"That she is the Fu Haizi kingpin?"

Hurst was calling it Fu Haizi now? "Yes. What do you think about that?"

"I think it's more important what you think about it."

"It's surreal."

"Not what you feel. What you think."

"Yes." It was more surreal to admit it out loud. So, she decided to say it again. "Yes, it makes more and more sense every time I think about it." They turned the last corner onto the highway that led to her home and Duncan's brother's place they liked to call the Reed Farm. "There's more."

"I was countin' on it."

"My mother's men didn't just wipe down her house. The NPD captain who resided before Dave Nolan was involved."

"I remember reading about that."

"I think she had him hanged. He was found in his cell this morning."

"Are you sure? Pedophiles aren't treated so well in prison."

"Private cell. I arranged it for him myself. Used it to bribe him for information whenever I needed it. His wrists had raw abrasions around them."

Hurst nodded as he followed the Jag onto the drive leading to Andy's place.

"And Phil the barber's place."

"The meeting spot in downtown Northridge? The one with the guns?"

"Yes. An informant of mine tipped me off." Did she just call Slippery 'Scumbag' Jimbo her informant? It stuck to her mouth coming out. "He took a nasty beating for me at the hands of Jun Zheng. His tip helped me find a hidden door leading to a basement."

"Let me guess. With mattresses and cages."

"Just been emptied of them."

"So, your version of transparency," he said, making quotation marks in the air with his fingers, "is meeting with this imprisoned captain and searching Phil the barber's shop without me?"

"I didn't know if I could trust you."

"Yeah. I get that, Nick. I get that."

When they reached the end of the drive, Nickie spotted Eddy leaning on the hood of his unmarked. Jimbo was still in the back. Andy and Rose were there. Nickie closed her eyes. How she did not want to get them involved. Rose had A.J. in her arms.

Hurst pulled in next to Duncan. As they got closer, Nickie realized the thing in Rose's arms wasn't a kid. "That's the map," she said to Hurst.

"This map thing is real?"

She scrunched her eyebrows. "Hey!"

"You gotta admit it sounded like potential bullshit used to keep you in the know."

"Okay, okay." As soon as he stopped, she opened the car door but then paused. Transparency. Hurst saved her life. He deserved it. "I've wanted to take another look at this map. The locations we discovered are turning out to be former spots where Fu Haizi kept groups of captive children. My parents' home. I went and checked out Henderson, Nevada. It's been empty since the take down last year."

"You went to Henderson, Nevada, without telling me, too?"

Oops. She slinked out of the SUV and walked to the group. Duncan was pulling Parker out of his Jag by the arm. His leg was wrapped like a mummy, as well as his nose and arm. That and the hospital gown made him look like they kidnapped him before he was ready. Since that was the honest truth, Nickie decided not to explain this to Andy and Rose.

The looks on their faces as they stared at Parker said they didn't want to know.

"Brother," Andy said and gave Duncan a one-armed hug and smack on the back. "I got out the map like you asked. You sure you want to show these dudes?" Andy's gaze moved from Parker to Jimbo in the back of Eddy's car.

"I am."

"Your call," Andy said, shrugged and glanced over at Parker. "Horses are ready."

"Horses?" Parker yelled.

"Shut up," Duncan and Hurst said.

"No, don't shut up," Eddy said and strutted over to Parker. "You should know all about this map since you're the one who helped create it."

"I swear, sir." Parker held up his hands. "Ms. Jacobsen did the sending and receiving. I was the conduit, it's true, but I know very little about technology."

Before someone got hurt, Andy elbowed his way between Eddy and Parker and propped the map on the bumper of his pickup. "You see here," he said. "Each of these lines were traced from Detective Lynx's hacked station desktop computer and the planted laptop found in his apartment."

Andy ran a hand over one of the lines. It was one that went across the heart of the country. "This is a dummy trace sent from Baltimore to Henderson to Minneapolis before it hit Eddy's computer in Northridge. False leads."

"Each of these is a trace?" Hurst's gaze traveled over the hundreds of lines.

"Dummy trace. Set specifically."

"How long did this take you?"

Andy cocked his head toward Hurst. "See? Now, you get that."

"It's the holes." It was Duncan's voice from the back of the group.

"What are the holes?" Nickie asked.

"The locations. The hot spots. We've been looking at the places on the map where clusters of lines converge. Those are old locales. Henderson, Nevada. Baltimore, Maryland. When I was searching through the Leslie Jacobsen files, I remember mention of importing and exporting goods to Peru and Ontario. Northridge was also recorded." He stepped between Special Agent Hurst in his suit and shiny shoes and barefoot Parker in his hospital gown and robe.

Pointing one hand toward Canada and one toward South America. "I assumed the international locations were the legit side of the Monticello business and that Northridge was where the trace was headed. No lines touch those spots. In Andy's myriad of crisscrossing, the locations are holes. Circles of voids made from the absence of the trace lines."

Nickie stood back and scanned the entire map as a whole, purposely forcing her eyes to ignore the clusters of crisscrossing lines and taking mental note of the voids, or holes as Duncan described them. She noticed that one of these holes was over Northridge—Phil the barber's place.

CHAPTER 28

L egs spread, knees locked, Special Agent Hurst stood behind Parker as he sat on a log in his hospital robe. Andy had given him a pair of flip-flops to wear. After all the crap Parker had done to Nickie and Eddy, she would have rather he walked barefoot around the campfire site.

Since it was going to take a while for Duncan to show up with Xena, Nickie took her time making the fire. Dig under the wet leaves to find dry ones. Make a small pile. Stack a bunch of nice, dry sticks about pencil sized like a teepee. Place a few thicker ones on top of that. Collect some branches broken into two-foot pieces to add when the fire got good and hot.

She was going to owe Andy and Rose big for babysitting Slippery Jimbo while she interrogated Parker at the campsite.

Parker jumped at every squirrel, bird and chipmunk that scurried by. It made her happy.

"Where the fuck are we?" he demanded and began to stand. "I told you I would cooperate."

"No, you didn't," Hurst said, placing his hands on his shoulders and shoving him back down.

"I planted the laptop in Lynx's apartment. I pried open his front door and planted it. I've been sending the emails."

Hurst moved his fingers over the gunshot wound in Parker's shoulder and pressed. Through Parker's wails, Hurst said, "We already know that, dumbass."

She spotted Duncan making his way through the trees. Their home was far enough up the hill she assumed Xena wouldn't catch the scent of Parker until they were closer. She was wrong. The girl came tearing through the woods, zigzagging between the trees in as straight of a line as she could, heading for Parker.

As soon as Parker spotted her, he howled, "Goodrich hired me to send the emails. He planted the bug!"

"No shit," Hurst said, hovering his fingers over the gunshot wound. "Tell us something we don't already know, or I massage your bullet hole again."

"I know that you're in over your head. You have no idea—" He shuddered at Xena's growl as she came closer. "—what you're dealing with."

Nickie rolled her eyes and lit the dry leaves with a match. "Yeah, yeah, yeah. So people keep telling us. You know what I do know? I know that you're in deep shit. Your boss wants you dead. Enough to send two—count them, two—federal moles out to do the job."

"Preaching to the choir."

"I get that. I can keep you in a safe house."

"There is no safe place."

"Do you see any Fu Haizi out here?"

Nickie lifted a single brow just as Xena cleared the brush. "Xena, sit," Nickie commanded. Xena whimpered and stopped, but she didn't sit. Her growl was low and angry, foam trickled from the corners of her mouth.

"Xena, sit," she repeated. The pup obeyed but kept her gaze and snout facing Parker.

Time to go out on a limb and trust the profiler. It might kill Nickie to do it. Or possibly ruin her bluff. She paced and waved her hand in the air like a conductor. "My mother is the ring leader. Zheng is her pawn. Blah, blah, blah."

She took a moment and stopped pacing. Through the thick trees around her, she pictured Duncan's aunt trimming the overgrown limbs. "They're rebuilding their groups of children since yours truly cut back those groups. I'm going to chainsaw the trunk of Fu Haizi and let her fall." She turned to face Parker. "I have a safe house for you." Or Duncan does anyway.

She stepped in front of him and lifted his chin. "If you have something for me."

His eyes met hers. "They have groups of kids all over the country."

"Already knew that. Not helpful." Nickie began pacing again toward the growing fire.

"They aren't all groups of girls."

"Some boys," she said. "Some girls. Some young. Some not so young. I'm losing my patience. Xena," Nickie called.

Duncan held her collar as she growled and lunged forward. Such a good doggie.

"I want names and addresses."

"I hear them talking about Peru," he yelled and covered his bandaged face with his arms. "They talk about it like it's some kind of headquarters."

Nickie looked to Duncan. Duncan placed a spread hand a few feet in front of Xena, who reluctantly sat her butt down. Duncan glanced up to Hurst, who nodded.

Sensing the fun was over, Xena took it upon herself to lie on the leaves, stuck her tongue out and panted near the fire.

Hurst walked around the log and looked Parker in the eyes. "You testify against Edward and Ivanna Monticello and against Jun Zheng, tell us what you know about Peru and we'll hook you up in a rock solid witness protection plan."

Parker nodded and sighed. "Pardon me if I don't have faith. Keep your eyes open, Detective."

She really wished people would quit telling her that. Xena lifted her nose, craned her head and bolted from Duncan's grip.

"Xena, come," he boomed. She ignored him like he hadn't spoken.

"Hey, I thought that dog was trained," Parker yelled.

"Shut up, backstabber. She is," Nickie said and lowered her brows at Duncan. "I'll go after her. It's my turn."

"No." Duncan held her arm. "Get Parker out of here." He took off running after Xena.

"Like hell," Duncan heard Nickie yell as he sprinted after his dog. He hoped Xena was running after an irresistible herd of deer. It had happened before, but something scratched at the back of his mind, telling him this was no animal of the four-legged kind.

There was no reason to attempt a covert approach. Xena's barking announced to the world they were coming. Gun drawn, Duncan sprinted over the leaves, fully upright and dodging saplings as he went.

Explosives. If there was a smell Duncan would never forget, it was explosives. It didn't take an eidetic memory but years serving as an expert on the front line. The rumble of igniting engines in his driveway caused him to change course in that direction.

As Duncan cleared the corner of his home, he noted six SUVs lined in two rows of three, facing the highway. Men in black mock turtlenecks disappeared behind the closing shiny black doors. Xena ran after them. "Xena, no," Duncan yelled to deaf ears.

Behind one of the bigger boulders on the property, he dropped to one knee and took aim. He shot out the tires of the two in back. Pop, pop. A screech of the tires on the asphalt sounded from the first in the line. Pop, pop. Pop, pop, pop. Those were not from his gun.

Nickie and Special Agent Hurst had run in low, stopped behind some trees to the south of Duncan and opened fire. Eddy and Andy were coming around the west of Duncan's home, approaching from the back.

He hoped it wasn't all a hallucination or flashback and ducked and fell back on his heels. As his arms dangled to his sides, his Beretta fell to the ground. He tried clasping his eyes shut and chanted to himself. He was not in the desert. He was not wearing fatigues. He was on the wet grass of his home in upstate New York.

The smells of gunpowder. The sounds of continued gunfire. They opened fire on the vehicles, disabling four of the six of them.

Doors from the vehicles on the far side opened. Feet appeared beneath. Duncan looked to the ground at his gun that lay uselessly as he heard one of them yell, "It's going to blow!"

What was going to blow, Duncan wondered just as deafening blasts erupted behind him. Multiple discharges, one after another, blew out the windows of his home, his doors.

The body of his dog flew like a rag doll, smashing against the back of one of the SUVs, then landed on the asphalt and rolled on a pile of shattered glass.

Blasts and booms erupted around him. None of it mattered. His mind zeroed in on his Xena. It was a picture he would never forget. Her tongue lolling from the side of her mouth, and a drip of blood running from her nose. She'd been vulnerable. She was his. He had failed her.

More pops. More gunfire. More commands yelled from both sides.

"Duncan, please! Move!" Nickie's voice pulled him back to the present. He picked up his gun, rolled from his spot and shot round after round of ammo at the feet in his sight between the tires. Howls of pain erupted as three bodies fell. Next to him, the heat from the flames that engulfed his house burned the side of his face.

Sirens approached from the distance. Duncan knew they were from black and whites, but his subconscious heard airstrike sirens from the tops of stone buildings set on the sand. The heat. The flames. The gunfire. His Nickie.

His Nickie. He spotted her going in low toward Xena. A man in black darted and rolled toward her from around the front of one of the bullet-filled SUVs. Duncan took aim and shot him in the shoulder, knocking the gun from his hand. He fell on top of one of the other downed men a few yards from Nickie.

Gunfire ceased.

The lack of movement from around the shattered glass and mangled black metal was in direct contrast to the mass hysteria consuming his house. Ignoring the flames, he made his way to his wife as she slid over the messy pavement to their dog. She dropped her ear to her mouth, then moved it to her chest.

Nickie wrapped her arms around Xena and rocked.

Guns drawn, Duncan, Hurst and Eddy closed in. Moans and grumbles came from the injured as they rolled in pain over the gravel around and in the vehicles. His eyes darted from one to the other, watching for a weapon or danger.

A figure came sprinting from the west side of Duncan's burning home. He spun his aim in the direction of the movement. It was James. He ran with his light brown trench coat flapping behind him. Maneuvering around the vehicles, Duncan saw what James chased. One of the perps slipped away on all fours. James landed on him and pounded him with one blow after another.

With Hurst and Eddy to cover him, Duncan ran the rest of the way to Nickie. He dropped to his knees and wrapped his arms around her as she wrapped hers around their pup.

CHAPTER 29

On the first floor of the police station, Nickie stood between the only two conference rooms in the building. "Are you sure this is okay?" she asked. Jess Larsen, co-founder of Child Rescue stood next to her.

He folded his arms and nodded. "It's unconventional, not that any of this was conventional. But for you, yes."

In one room a training session began for the NPD officers and detectives as well as the men in blue from surrounding counties. An anonymous donor had paid for it. She looked to Duncan. He winked.

NPD was one of the lucky ones. Budgets no longer afforded this kind of training. It provided strategies and options available for women and children as victims of trafficking rather than treated as prostitutes. A safe house for rehab instead of juvie.

The unconventional part came with the others who attended the class. Duncan's brother, Andy, and Andy's wife, Rose. His aunt and uncle, Brie and Nathan. And Nickie's foster family, Gloria, Gil and Teresa. Each had browbeaten her into attending. It was the least Nickie could do since she refused to bring them along to confront her father as she'd promised.

They pushed their way into Nickie's past, present and

future. She smiled as she scanned the room. She needed them to be safe. This wouldn't keep them from a bullet, but it would bring them that much closer to knowledge. And knowledge was power.

The young Nevaeh Thornton led a group in the adjoining room. College students. Her age. Nickie didn't know of any who were victims of rape as Nevaeh was. Or maybe they were. All Nickie knew was that she was as proud as if Nevaeh were her daughter.

The class was a training session of a different kind. Nevaeh was teaching college students to be trainers. They would, in turn, teach high school and college girls safety strategies to prevent rape or abduction. Duncan described it as a small ripple in the water of a calm pond.

Duncan.

He stood on the other side of her with Xena sitting next to him. Until the girl's ribs healed, he wouldn't leave her side. Broken from the force of the explosion onto the Fu Haizi SUV, she sat wagging her tail.

Nickie stepped closer to him and inhaled his scent. His presence was like a battery giving her the energy to go on. "I'm really tired of having your house blown up because of me," she whispered.

"Our house," he corrected, "and not because of you, but because of Fu Haizi." He kissed the top of her head. "Brick and mortar is just that. We have each other, our Xena and family." He gestured toward the group of faithful people who loved them enough to be present that day.

"Will we ever stop them?"

"The hydra has many heads," he said. "We've cut off Jun Zheng and Dale Parker. We destroyed a fleet of their vehicles and arrested over a dozen of their men in their failed attempt to steal intel and intimidate us. We have your father in custody. It's only a matter of time until we have the rest of them stuffed and mounted on a wall." He laced his fingers in hers. "Our time is coming, my Nickie. This isn't over yet."

*Turn the page for an
excerpt from*

SAVAGE
ALLIANCE

The Nickie Savage Series
Book Five

R.T. Wolfe

Dozens of patrons crowded the corridors. The museum accommodated the number with ease, but that did little to placate Duncan Reed. While greeting his admirers, he scanned faces and evaluated tuxedo jackets for hidden weapons.

His landscapes and still lifes replaced the customary artwork and would be on display through the following week. However, since tonight's event doubled as a fundraiser, Duncan reminded himself to be cordial.

He and one of the attendees locked eyes. The mayor of Las Vegas. Duncan nodded toward him as he stepped around a smaller portrait. It sat on an easel next to one of the massive marble beams that broke up the area. The mayor was safe. The subject of the portrait was not.

Oscar awarding winning actress, Coral Francesca, didn't pose the kind of threat Duncan feared that evening. Nonetheless, a threat she was. Since she slithered her way toward him at that moment, he stopped and raised his guard.

He had been on her arm the evening she won Best Supporting Actress. It was one of many events that netted him the label, Taste of L.A. Crooking her wrist, she closed the space between them and placed her forefinger on his shoulder. After a telling pause, she slid it down the arm of his tuxedo. "I'm terribly sorry to hear about the fire, dear." She shook her head and tsk'd. "Such a shame. I hope you didn't lose everything."

His everything appeared from around a corner. He lifted the side of his mouth. The difference between the two women caused him to accept a more sensible view of the fire's results. He may be temporarily living in a hotel, but his wife and family were unharmed. The crime ring responsible was depleted and on the run.

Coral glanced over her shoulder at the subject of his grin. His Nickie glided across the floor in an ivory sequined, tea-length gown. He'd purchased it for her during an undercover operation. The back was high enough to cover her scars. In contrast, Coral's dress was fire-engine red, a halter gown that exposed her back from the clasp at her neck to just above her buttocks.

Nickie smiled and greeted each patron with a raised ivory-gloved hand. The gliding and the gloved hand—they was necessary. He understood this. However, he preferred her as the unrefined Detective Nickie Savage. A brassy, complicated and selfless woman who wore black boots, tight pants and often spoke like a sailor. Although he appreciated each hat she wore, tonight's hat was rather disconcerting.

"Hello, Coral," Nickie said as she approached. "Thank you for coming to the fundraiser this evening. I do hope you're hungry."

"Oh goodie," Coral said and checked the backs of her nails. "Small town food."

Nickie dropped her chin and nodded. "If you're worried about the menu, no need. I believe the chef has prepared a red-wine braised duck with capers and lemon." She smiled and tilted her head. "If you're just being a bitch, don't eat."

Coral rolled her eyes. "I see Johnny and Bebe. I think I'll make my way to more suitable conversation." She rotated on the balls of her five-inch heeled ice-pick sandals and slithered away as slowly as she'd approached.

Nickie's smile faded. "I shouldn't have done that."

"It was the highlight of my evening," he said and brought her gloved fingers to his lips.

She lifted her chin and pulled her shoulders back. "Tonight is important. The ticket price has a friggin' comma in it. I can't believe how many people showed up."

Her poised posture may have been unnerving, but at least she spoke like his Nickie.

"Child Rescue needs this money." She placed her hand over his heart. "Thank you. This is going to fund their next jump team to Central America. It could help rescue dozens of children."

"You're welcome. Let us get through the evening. We leave first thing in the morning to start our search for Fu Haizi. You are right to begin your search for the rest of the organization in their weakened state."

"Or I just thought it was a good time to go since we're homeless and all."

A cell phone rang.

"Nickie, my wife," Duncan said. "Your dress is ringing."

Nickie blushed as she reached between her breasts to retrieve her cell. "Savage," she said into it and turned away. "How many children? The Belmont Stakes? That's tomorrow."

Duncan looked around. Dozens of people were here to view his work and donate to Child Rescue. He was the host of honor.

"I'll be right there," she said and spun to face him, an apologetic expression written over her face.

They exchanged a silent conversation before he gestured toward the back door. She nodded and slid her hand in his.

SAVAGE ALLIANCE

available in print and ebook

THE NICKIE SAVAGE SERIES

Savage Echoes

Savage Deception

Savage Rendezvous

Savage Disclosure

Savage Betrayal

Savage Alliance

R.T. Wolfe enjoys creating diverse characters, twining them together in the midst of an intelligent mystery and a heart encompassing romance. It's not uncommon to find dark chocolate squares in R.T.'s candy dish, her rescued Saint Bernard at her feet and a few caterpillars spinning their cocoons in their terrariums on her counters. R.T. loves her family, gardening, eagle-watching and can occasionally be found in a third world country helping others help themselves.

R.T. enjoys hearing from readers. You can contact R.T. through her website: www.rtwolfe.com

www.ingramcontent.com/pod-product-compliance
Lightning Source LLC
Chambersburg PA
CBHW050520260626
47157CB00004B/1404